Jackson's Woman

MAGGIE PRICE

KU-433-694

MILLS & BOON®

Pure reading pleasure™

First published in Great Britain 2008
by Harlequin Mills & Boon Limited,
Eton House, 18-24 Paradise Road, Richmond, Surrey TW9 1SR

© Margaret Price 2007

ISBN: 978 0 263 85978 2

46-0708

Harlequin Mills & Boon policy is to use papers that are natural, renewable and recyclable products and made from wood grown in sustainable forests. The logging and manufacturing processes conform to the legal environmental regulations of the country of origin.

Printed and bound in Spain
by Litografia Rosés S.A., Barcelona

ABOUT THE AUTHOR

Before embarking on a writing career, Maggie Price took a walk on the wild side and started associating with people who carry guns. Fortunately they were cops, and Maggie's career as a crime analyst with the Oklahoma City Police Department has given her the background needed to write true-to-life police procedural romances, which have won numerous accolades, including a nomination for the coveted RITA® Award.

Maggie is a recipient of a Golden Heart Award, a Career Achievement Award from *Romantic Times BOOKreviews*, a National Reader's Choice Award and a Bookseller's Best Award, all in series romantic suspense. Readers are invited to contact Maggie at 416 NW 8th St, Oklahoma City, OK 73102-2604, USA. Or on the web at www.MaggiePrice.net.

To "old" friends Mary Nichols Denson and Karen Westfall Perez, with thanks for the warm memories, the great sleepovers, the triple dates and all the dreams we used to weave.

Prologue

The dark-haired geologist who swung open the door to his favorite Barcelona restaurant was tall, lean and lanky, in the prime of his life.

In five minutes, he'd be dead.

At the tree-shaded park a safe distance away, a man fueled by cold revenge stabbed a button on his cell phone.

"Target's in." Without waiting for a reply, he ended the call.

Through powerful binoculars the man scanned the lunchtime crowd jamming the sunny sidewalk in front of the restaurant. When he spotted the two blond women who'd paused to check the menu posted outside the restaurant, his throat closed. Each dressed in a bright sundress, their skin tanned, they looked so much like his wife and teenage daughter he felt a wave of nausea. Sweat beaded his forehead, his palms.

Don't go inside. The warning flashed in his brain while fresh grief that was beyond name, beyond reason, ripped at his gut.

The older of the two women pointed at something on the menu and shook her head; the younger one shrugged. They continued down the sidewalk, skirts swishing against tanned legs, neither knowing that the decision to bypass the restaurant had saved their lives.

Layer by layer, he rebuilt control so that his hands were rock-steady when the teenager with friendly brown eyes appeared around the corner. The kid was solidly built, wearing jeans and a red T-shirt.

No reason for anyone watching him to suspect that the blue backpack hanging over one shoulder held a deadly device.

The teen tugged open the restaurant's door and stepped inside. Minutes later he strolled out, sans backpack.

The man turned and headed for the far side of the park, the soles of his scuffed boots silent on the thick grass. He was three blocks away when the deafening blast rocked the air. Even from a distance, he could hear agonized screams.

His stomach clenched as the memory of other screams razored through him. He'd arrived at the safe house too late, had no choice but to stay hidden while listening to his wife and daughter scream before they died.

They'd been gone two weeks. Two weeks of despair, confusion and agony.

Now, a feral tangle of rage and hate and revenge drove him to make the bastard responsible for their deaths pay.

Today he had accomplished the first step toward that goal.

Jackson Castle's twin brother was dead.

His woman would die next.

Eye for an eye.

Chapter 1

Good to be home, Claire Munroe thought while juggling her purse, overnight bag, keys and one of the cardboard boxes containing the finds she couldn't wait to display in her antique shop. It was late—all the businesses in Oklahoma City's Reunion Square had closed hours ago—so she'd parked at the curb, a few feet from Home Treasures' entrance. Smart move, she decided, since the temperature hovered in the eighties and the box weighed a ton.

In the hushed darkness there was only the click of her sandals on concrete as she lugged everything across the sidewalk.

Thankful for the carriage lamps that cast puddles of light on the shop's entryway, she managed to slide her key into the lock on the first try. The dead bolt snicked open; when the door swung inward she was greeted by cool air and the scent of the apple and pine potpourri she'd placed all around. A wash of weak light glowed from the pair of timer-operated globe lamps that went on each evening at dusk.

She had been away for only one night, but to a woman who'd sacrificed so much to own the building that housed her shop and the cozy apartment over it, even that short time away had been too long.

Balancing the box against one hip, she turned, intending to punch her code into the alarm panel, but hesitated when she saw the glowing green light indicating the system wasn't armed. Glancing across her shoulder, her gaze swept the dim shop with its lofty ceiling. Curio cabinets loaded with salt cellars, fragile teacups and enameled boxes sat exactly where she'd left them. Nearby, the mahogany table topped by a small antique chest and a collection of pewter ale mugs appeared just as it had when she'd locked up the previous evening and set the alarm.

Claire sighed. This was the third time she'd come home and found her alarm unarmed after arranging for her handyman to do repairs while the shop was closed. Silas Smith was in his late seventies and getting forgetful. At least the sweet old man had remembered to lock the dead bolt.

Using the tip of one sandal, Claire shoved the door closed. She slid her keys into a back pocket of her jeans, relocked the door and headed toward the rear of the shop. She had one more box to retrieve from her SUV, then she would set the alarm and head upstairs. Topping her agenda was a hot soak in the tub accompanied by a glass of chilled wine.

All thought of that agenda flew out of her head when her foot rammed into something solid, sending her lurching forward. The weight of the box added to her body's momentum and she went down hard, her right side slamming against the box's top edge.

The impact knocked the breath out of her. Everything went dim for a moment, like a blown fuse snapping off all the lights.

Claire remained motionless until her vision cleared. Her breath shuddered out. Then in. Slowly, she eased into a sitting position, wincing against the pain in her ribs.

Whatever she'd tripped over hadn't been there when she'd locked up her shop the previous evening. Shoving her hair out of her face, she looked over her shoulder.

Her eyes went wide when she saw the leg that jutted into the aisle. It was khaki-clad and wore a heavy, paint-spattered work boot that she recognized.

"Mr. Smith?" Claire asked, scooting toward her handyman.

He was sprawled on one side, his back to her. The thick gray hair that always gleamed like silver looked dull in the shadowy light.

"Mr. Smith?" Claire repeated, her voice thready.

He had a bad heart, had suffered a heart attack the previous year. Fingers unsteady, she leaned across his body and touched his hand. His flesh was ice-cold.

"Oh, no." She closed her eyes. He hadn't turned on the alarm because he'd never left the shop. Had the poor man lain here for hours, suffering, needing help before he died?

Heartsick, Claire pushed to her feet, flinching at the catch in her side. She needed to call the police. Her cell phone was in her purse, which had gone airborne when she fell.

She flicked on a nearby lamp. When she leaned to retrieve her purse, a weak sweep of light illuminated the handyman's pale face…and the gaping, bloody slit across his throat. Her brain frozen with shock, Claire stared at the dark crimson that had pooled from the wound.

Then reality hit with a hard jolt and she pressed a hand to her mouth to hold back a scream. All at once the air around her felt too cold. Too quiet. And then she heard a faint creak, the way a floorboard protested weight, that seemed to come from above. From her apartment.

Oh, God! Oh, God!

Hair rising on the back of her neck, the sensation of another presence clamped like fingers around her throat. No way was she staying here to find out if Silas Smith's killer was upstairs, waiting for her with his bloody knife.

She spun, raced toward the front door. Her heartbeat battled her aching ribs, her temples pounded while her trembling hands fought the dead bolt. Jerking the door open, she darted out into the night that now seemed thick with shadows.

Five feet from the door a dark form stepped into her path so suddenly Claire didn't have a chance to evade, much less stop. Sandals skidding, she rammed into a solid, unyielding frame.

The collision dragged a shriek from her. The hands that locked onto her shoulders were all that kept her on her feet.

"What the hell?"

The deep voice barely registered past the roar of blood in Claire's ears. She recoiled against the man's grip, but she was no match for the iron strength she felt in his hands. All she could see was a face awash in shadows; all she could think was the hands now controlling her were the same ones that had sliced her handyman's throat.

"Let go!"

Blinding terror and the honed instincts of a child who'd grown up warding off advances from her mother's numerous boyfriends blasted through Claire. Teeth bared, she bunched her right hand into a fist and swung. Her knuckles connected with his jaw, snapping his head back.

He grunted. In the next instant, he spun her around, jerked her back and trapped her against his hard, rock-solid body.

With her arms locked against her sides, she kicked, her heel ramming into his shin. "Let go!"

"Dammit, Claire, it's *me*."

She went rigid. No, it can't be. She was so scared, she was hallucinating because there was *no way* she could be struggling in the thick shadows with the man from whom she'd walked away two years ago.

But the familiar scent of musky aftershave and potent male told her different.

"Let…go." It was no longer solely fear that had her fighting his hold, but also shock and a desperate need to see if it was really *him*.

He kept her captured against the hard press of his body a second longer, then released her. She whirled, and in the weak wash from a carriage lamp she stared up into Jackson Castle's hard blue gaze.

Her lungs heaved. Her throat was locked so tight she couldn't speak. How could this be real?

"Jackson…" she finally managed.

His eyes swept up and down the street. "What the hell's going on?" he asked in an almost inaudible whisper. "Who are you running from?"

"I…" She took a step backward, then another. He was dressed in black jeans and a black T-shirt, making him difficult to see; only his bare arms, hands and face made him visible. She strained to get a better look at his face, but the shadows were too heavy. "What are you doing here?"

"Tell me who you're running from," he demanded.

"I…don't know." She fought to think past her shocked disbelief from finding her handyman murdered and plowing into Jackson Castle on her doorstep. Then her thoughts careened in on what he did for a living and she took a stumbling step backward.

"Did…you…have anything to do with that?"

"With what?"

"With…. With…. Oh, God!"

He closed the space between them, his hands locking on her shoulders again, tight, giving her a shake. "Claire, tell me what happened."

"He's dead!" she blurted in a voice that even to her own ears sounded far away. "Inside. Someone slit his throat."

Jackson's right hand shifted from her shoulder. "Who's dead?"

"Silas!"

She didn't see Jackson reach for it, but now he held a pistol pressed against his thigh. Her heart pounded even harder. His job required that he always carry a gun, but she'd never gotten used to that. Had been unable to get used to a lot of things about Jackson Castle's lifestyle. "Jackson, what the hell are you doing here?"

His fingers tightened on her shoulder. "Who is Silas?"

"Silas Smith. My handyman."

"Did you see who killed him?"

"No. I...just got home...and found him. I might have heard someone upstairs in my apartment." She shook her head. "I'm not sure, it could have been the building settling."

His mouth tightened. "Is the key to the inside staircase in the same place?"

Claire blinked. Of course Jackson remembered the key. He'd been *trained* to recall every detail of everything he experienced. Things like that came in handy for a man who, in addition to other duties, slipped like smoke in and out of foreign countries to deal with rebels, terrorists and fanatics.

"The key's still where it was, but there's no reason for you to go into the building." Her voice shook. "If you have your cell phone, we can call the police. I have a friend who works homicide. We can call Liz, wait for her to get here."

"After I check the building," he said flatly.

No way was Jackson going to let a possible suspect escape. And he had a good idea who that suspect might be. He had no proof Frank Ryker had managed to get into the country, much less make it to Oklahoma City. Nor would someone with his training have to resort to throat-slicing to take out a handyman. But these days his mentor and former partner was operating on icy adrenaline and hot lust for revenge so Jackson wasn't taking chances. Not when Ryker's ultimate goal was to kill Claire. In case he was here, Jackson had no intention of giving him a chance to melt into the night before the local law arrived.

He looked back at Claire, his cop's mind assessing her condition. In the dim light her skin looked ashen, her eyes glassy with shock. She trembled outwardly. He set his jaw, wishing he had time to explain what was going on, but the danger was too great.

He did a quick surveil of the area. All the shops, restaurants and other businesses in the square were closed, so he couldn't stash Claire in one of them while he checked her building. His rental car was parked behind her shop; he'd kept tabs on her enough to know she owned the SUV sitting at the front curb. He quickly nixed the idea of having her lock herself inside either vehicle and wait for him. If Ryker was around, it would take him only seconds to bypass any lock system. And then he'd have Claire.

And kill her.

Jaw set, Jackson leaned in, keeping his voice low. "I'm going to check your building—"

"You're not leaving me here on the sidewalk," she interrupted in a harsh whisper. "You've got the gun, I'm sticking with you."

Even in the shadows he saw the determined glint in

her eyes. Too bad she hadn't been this adamant about "sticking with him" two years ago. Would regret, he wondered, ever fade?

"I'm not leaving you out here," he agreed. "You're going in with me. *Behind* me. Don't make any noise. At the first loud sound, hit the floor."

Her eyes widened, flicked to his automatic. "Loud sound, meaning gunfire?"

"Meaning anything. Don't get too close in case I have to step back fast." *And so you don't get hit by shots aimed at me,* he added to himself. "Once we're inside, I want you to stay in my line of sight so I'll know where you are. Keep glancing over your shoulder to make sure no one sneaks up on us from behind."

"All right." Claire pressed a palm against the ache in her right side and pulled in a trembling breath. Her nerves were shimmering and her insides had tangled into a dozen frayed knots.

"Jackson, I don't understand why you're here," she said in a shaky whisper. "Why are you even here?"

"To check on you."

His gaze was unreadable, his tone as offhand as if he'd just driven across the city to get there when chances were he'd woken up that morning on some other continent. Every move the man made, everything he did was deliberate. She knew damn well his checking on her was far from casual.

"Stay close." He gave her shoulder a squeeze, then stepped past her, holding the automatic against his thigh.

Silently, he positioned himself at one side of the shop's gaping front door.

For Claire, the whole night had turned surreal. Within the past five minutes she'd found her handyman murdered and literally run head-first into the man who'd once embraced her heart as no other had. The man she had never thought she would see again.

Had never *wanted* to see again. Because she'd known, in her heart, how much it would hurt to be reminded of what she'd sacrificed in order to obtain her one solid goal: A life with permanence, where people stayed in one place and put down roots.

She'd been right.

She met his grim gaze while her heart tattooed in her ears. "Jackson, be careful."

One side of his mouth lifted. "That's my plan."

Gun clenched in both hands, he flattened his back against the door frame, then stepped inside.

Claire couldn't stop pacing.

Left hand pressed against her aching ribs, she roamed the living room of her spacious, high-ceilinged apartment. There was too much tension racing through her blood for her to sit still. The horrific image of Silas Smith with his throat a bloody gash. Her grief over the dear, sweet man's violent death. Her shock at running full-throttle into Jackson Castle.

Immediately after the surreptitious—and uneventful—search she and Jackson had conducted of her shop, her upstairs apartment and the storage room across the

hall, he'd pulled out his cell phone and called 9-1-1. A
patrol car had arrived minutes later. Claire's friend,
Oklahoma City Police Department homicide detective
Elizabeth Scott, her partner and the crime scene investi-
gators soon followed, and the medical examiner showed
up shortly afterward.

With so much going on and so many people swarming
her building, Claire had yet to find an opportune moment
to talk to Jackson one on one.

Diverting around her couch that bloomed with small
pink roses, she glanced across the room. He stood just
inside the apartment's open front door, talking in muted
tones to Liz, who had already questioned Claire at length.
And since her partner had sat in, Liz had held back from
asking certain girlfriend-type questions, the most pressing being: why had the lover Claire walked away from
two years ago suddenly shown up tonight?

Claire wished to hell she knew.

Sidestepping the pedestal table that held china cups on
a silver tray, she continued pacing. Out of the corner of
her eye, she watched Liz jot on a notepad, then return a
small leather case to Jackson. Claire knew the case held
the badge and credentials that identified him as a Special
Agent with the Diplomatic Security Service—the U.S.
State Department's law-enforcement division.

Had he shown Liz his ID because his presence here
was official? Claire wondered. If so, what sort of business
had prompted a DSS agent who mostly operated under a
veil of secrecy in foreign countries to suddenly show up
on the shadowy sidewalk in front of her building?

The building Claire had worked tooth and nail to own, along with the contents of the antique shop and the cozy apartment she and her aunt had once rented.

The apartment that was the only real home Claire had ever known.

Over the past two years, she had morphed Home Treasures to reflect her own personal stamp and was making a tidy profit. She'd met a man for whom she cared deeply, a man who loved her, who wanted a future with her. Brice Harrison had been ready—was ready—to give her the type of life craved by a woman who'd survived a rootless childhood that hovered one frightening step from physical abuse. Claire had nearly convinced herself to grab onto that life. To write off her growing uncertainties and her frustrating inability to totally forget the past.

And the man who'd played such a large role in it.

Dammit, why was he here?

Claire reached the fireplace—filled for summer with lavender hydrangea blooms—reversed and headed back the way she'd come. It was a wonder her sandals hadn't worn a trail across the Multan rug that spread its muted colors over the hardwood floor.

She could understand Jackson's being in Oklahoma City—they'd first met while he was on loan to a multi-agency anti-terrorism task force working out of the National Memorial Institute. So it was possible a similar assignment had brought him back.

But that didn't explain why he'd shown up tonight. Especially since they'd agreed to sever all ties. So, why was he *here?*

And why did it have to be now, when she'd spent the past months feeling so unsettled? So unsure. So off-balance.

Slowing her pace, she shifted her gaze back to Jackson and for the first time allowed herself to study him. He seemed leaner and a little more rugged now. The dark stubble that covered his firm, square jaw enhanced the look, as did the black T-shirt that stretched over his broad shoulders and the black jeans that clung to his narrow hips and long legs. Though worn in the same sleek style, his dark hair was shaggier, the thick ends lapping just above his collar.

His incendiary blue eyes had undergone the greatest change. They stared out from a face baked copper by the sun of who-knew-what countries, their unfamiliar hardness lending their owner a rougher and even more dangerous look than Claire remembered. A paper-thin gash, still in the process of healing, sliced through his left eyebrow.

She pictured him as he'd looked earlier, searching the shop with measured care, moving like a ghost up the stairs, his gun unwavering in his grip, his gaze skimming, shifting. Even though the shop was brimming with stock, she would wager he could describe everything he had seen as skillfully as he would faces in a lineup. Even minor details didn't get past him.

As if sensing her thoughts, Jackson shifted his stance, met her gaze. His eyes held hers for a long moment, then dropped to the hand she held pressed against her ribs. A frown line formed between his dark brows.

A tightness settled in Claire's chest. Was he measuring

her the way she had him? Searching for physical changes in the woman who'd called it quits and left him after a passionate affair that had lasted only a handful of months?

"Claire?"

Halting beside the pedestal table, she shifted her gaze to her friend. "Yes?"

"We're wrapping things up downstairs," Liz said as she stepped farther into the apartment. Tall and leggy, she wore black slacks and a turquoise blazer that nipped her thin waist. As usual, her ginger-gold hair was plaited in a tight French braid.

Claire was aware of Jackson moving to stand a few feet away in front of the fireplace. Propping a shoulder against the mantel, he crossed his arms over his chest.

A whiff of the familiar spicy tang of his aftershave reached her. Claire set her jaw against the quick clutching in her belly. Her body was simply reacting to a known stimulus, she told herself. Nothing more.

Still, his scent had her mind scrolling backward in time. It had been summer when he'd first walked into Home Treasures. She'd just been a sales clerk when she looked up and saw a tall, intense man stride through the doorway. While he explained he needed a wedding gift for a co-worker, she had felt the sexual attraction sparking between them, running like a sizzling conduit beneath the surface of every word they exchanged. The way Jackson's eyes had deepened, darkened, verified he felt it, too. They went out to dinner that night. And the next. Days later, Claire linked her fingers with his while they climbed the stairs to this very apartment. They'd cranked the air con-

ditioning to arctic, lit a fire and made love for hours while
flames danced on the logs.

And when the task force had disbanded and he'd asked
her to go with him, she'd said yes. Because she'd been
so crazy in love she couldn't bear to think about living
her life without Jackson Castle in it.

It had taken six months to learn that making life-
altering decisions based on one's hormones was for the
young and foolish. She was older now. Wiser. More
practical. Never again would she put aside her own
needs so rashly.

Her throat dry, she switched her mental focus to what
Liz was saying.

"...and we dusted for prints only on the displays
where things weren't in the same place you said they'd
been yesterday evening when you closed the shop. I
asked the lab guys to be careful with the fingerprint
powder, but you still have a mess to clean up."

Claire pictured the blood that had pooled from beneath poor Silas Smith's head. She had more than just
fingerprint powder to deal with. "I doubt I'll be able to
sleep tonight so cleaning the shop will give me something to do."

Her gaze concerned, Liz squeezed Claire's arm. "My
partner and I will be back in the morning to interview the
square's other business owners. Maybe one of them
caught a glimpse of someone hanging around outside
your shop. In the meantime, call me if you think of anything else that might be important. Or if you discover
anything missing from the building."

"All right." In reflex, Claire shifted her hand from the ache in her ribs to her throat. "Liz, do you have any idea at all who killed Silas?"

"Not yet. The alarm company says your system was deactivated using your code, so it's possible the suspect entered the shop after Mr. Smith turned off the alarm when he came in to do the repairs you wanted done. That's the most likely scenario."

"Do you have an unlikely one?"

"It's possible the suspect somehow obtained your code fraudulently, or had electronic equipment capable of cloning the code and disabling the system. Later, the victim walked in on him." Liz checked her notepad. "You're sure the only person other than yourself and Mr. Smith who has your alarm code is Charles?"

"Positive." Charles McDougal was much more to Claire than just Home Treasures' previous owner. When she was ten, she had come here to live with her aunt, and Charles and his late wife—who'd lived in the apartment across the hall—had opened their hearts to her.

Over the years, he had taught Claire all he knew about antiques. He'd helped send her to college, kept the apartment vacant for her when she'd run off with Jackson, and he'd welcomed her home when she'd returned with her heart broken.

Claire swallowed hard against that painful memory. "I always call Charles and let him know when I change my alarm code in case he drives through town when I'm not here."

When Liz frowned, Claire added, "You know how

concerned Charles is about my safety. There's no way he'd give my code to anyone."

"Not on purpose," Liz agreed. "I still need to make sure he didn't write down the latest code and leave it lying around where someone could see it. Do you know where he is now?"

Claire shook her head. The day the crusty widower had sold her the building and the shop's contents, he'd fired up his RV and taken off, vowing to stop at every antique shop, estate sale and flea market in the country.

"He called about a week ago from southern California. You should be able to reach him on his cell," Claire added and recited the number.

Liz slid her pad into a pocket. She looked at Jackson with the hard eyes of a cop, then shifted her gaze back to Claire.

"Special Agent Castle is here because he has a very different theory about the break-in and murder. Since I need to coordinate things with my partner and the lab guys, I'll let him explain it to you."

Instead of turning to go, Liz slid an arm around Claire's shoulders and gave her a hug. "I figure finding old Silas dead is just one of the shocks you've had tonight," she whispered.

Claire nodded. The other shock—Jackson's presence—was something to be discussed in detail later, girl-friend-to-girlfriend.

The cell phone clipped to Liz's waistband rang. She answered the call, spoke a few words then hung up. "Everything's done downstairs."

Claire pulled her keys from the back pocket of her jeans. "I'll walk you out and lock up."

She led the way down the inside stairway, acutely aware of Jackson trailing behind her and Liz.

At the bottom of the stairs, the door to the small room she used as an office stood open. Wordlessly, Claire passed by her tidy desk and file cabinet, then stepped into the shop where the lights blazed. She turned down one of the narrow aisles bordered by cloth-covered tables and display cases loaded with candlesticks, crystal bowls and vases. When she passed by the spot where she'd found poor Silas, her gaze lowered to the hardwood floor. The sight of the pool of dried blood had her stomach clenching while the apple- and pine-scented air cloyed in her lungs.

"Claire?" The deep timbre of Jackson's voice registered up and down her spine.

Pausing, she glanced across her shoulder. "Yes?"

"You still keep the cleaning supplies in the closet behind the main counter?"

She nodded. Did the man ever forget *anything?* "I don't expect you to help me clean."

"It'll go faster with two of us." He veered off toward the waist-high counter while she and Liz moved to the front door.

There, Liz turned, her eyes crimped with concern. "Look, I know what this guy once meant to you, but I'm a homicide cop and I don't take anyone at face value."

Claire felt her face pale. "You don't suspect Jackson…?"

"Not now that I've grilled him and checked out his credentials with the State Department." Liz flicked a look back at the closet behind the counter. "Considering the past you two share, it's gotta be hard for you to have him here. But if his theory's solid, I'm damn glad he *is* here."

Claire opened her mouth to ask what that theory was just as Liz's cell phone rang.

Muttering, Liz jerked it off her waistband and checked the display. "I've got to go. Call me if you need anything." Phone pressed to one ear, Liz headed out into the night.

Claire closed the door behind her friend, then engaged the dead bolt. From behind her came the rattle of the mop bucket.

It took a moment, a carefully indrawn breath, a steady exhale, before she turned. Her gaze tracked Jackson as he rolled the bucket containing a mop around the counter toward the spot where Silas had died.

"So, you have a theory about the break-in and murder," she began. "Is the reason you're here anything to do with what happened to Silas?"

Jackson positioned the bucket near the bloodstain, then leaned the mop's handle against the nearby white-washed pine armoire. "It's possible." He glanced again at the floor and frowned. "Not probable, but possible."

She took in the hard set of his jaw, his rigid shoulders. He hunted terrorists for a living. Was it possible Silas Smith's murder was an act of terrorism? The question might seem unbelievable if Reunion Square wasn't a short walk from the Oklahoma City Bombing Memorial. Like everyone else in the city, Claire had long ago abandoned the it-can't-happen-here mindset.

For the first time she noticed the shadows of fatigue

under Jackson's eyes and the small, pronounced lines at the corners of his mouth.

"Where were you when you woke up this morning?" she asked.

From somewhere blocks away came the shriek of a siren. Jackson turned his head, his gaze sweeping across the mullioned window that spanned the entire front of the shop. When he remet Claire's gaze, his eyes were intent, unnervingly watchful.

"I was in Spain."

"Did you travel most of today specifically to get here? Not just to Oklahoma City, but *here?*"

"Yes." He glanced at his watch. "I hopped a nonstop military transport. Taking the time change into consideration, I logged nearly eleven hours in the air."

She moved from the door, skirting several tables and displays before pausing a few feet from him. Beneath the shop's bright lights, the gash that slashed his left eyebrow looked even rawer. Claire didn't let herself try to imagine how he'd been injured. Or if he'd been in mortal danger at the time. She'd spent too many hours alone in various foreign countries while he was away on assignment, waiting for him to call, fearing he hadn't because he was lying dead in some place with a name she couldn't even pronounce.

"Are you saying you flew all those hours to get here because you suspected someone wanted to kill my handyman? Some homegrown terrorist? Someone like that?"

Jackson stepped toward her, halting when only inches separated them. His gaze narrowed, seemed to penetrate her.

"Yes," he said quietly, "I traveled today with the sole

intention of getting here, to you, as soon as I could. But it wasn't because I thought someone planned to slit your handyman's throat."

"Then why? Jackson, why are you here?"

"Because someone wants to kill *you*."

Chapter 2

Jackson watched Claire's face go pale and fear grow in her eyes. He gripped her upper arms. "It's not going to happen. I won't let it."

Beneath his hands, she swayed like a sheet in the wind. "Let's get you off your feet."

He hooked a foot around the leg of a chair and dragged it away from a table loaded with china and heavy silver. With a gentle push, he nudged her into the chair.

Dammit, he hadn't meant to tell her that way—after finding her handyman with his throat slit, the last thing she needed tonight was another shock. *Someone wants to kill you.* Smooth move, Castle.

When it came to his work, he was never at a loss. Didn't allow himself to get distracted from his focus.

But seeing Claire again had shaken him far more than he'd ever thought possible.

He ordered himself to snap back into control. *Now.* He couldn't have her. Logically he knew that. Shouldn't still want her. Didn't want to want her. He bit back on frustration. Too much was at stake for him to let the emotional baggage he'd dragged around since she'd walked out get in the way. Right now, Claire Munroe was a job—that's *all* she was. All she could be. Ryker had seen to that.

When she clutched the arms of the chair, Jackson crouched, putting them at eye-level. "Do you want some water? Something stronger?"

"I want an explanation." She let out a long breath, but it didn't steady her voice. "Who wants to kill me?"

He had found out less than twenty-four hours ago that she was in danger from a man he'd once considered his closest friend. He was still trying to come to grips with that. And everything else.

"Frank Ryker."

"I don't know him. Why would someone I don't know…" Her forehead furrowed. "*Ryker.* Isn't that your partner's last name? The man you consider your mentor?"

"Frank Ryker's my ex-partner, as of a little over a month ago."

"A federal cop, *your partner,* wants to kill me?" There was dismay in her voice now and color was returning to her cheeks. The tight grip she had on the arms of the chair had turned her knuckles white.

"Ex-partner, yes."

"Why?"

Because of me. His gut twisting, Jackson rose. After Claire had left him, he'd tried to put her out of his mind, and sometimes succeeded. But then he would come off an assignment and let go of the tight control necessary to survival on the job. It was at those times when he eased back his focus that thoughts of her closed in. They hovered around him like ghosts, whispering to him, brushing against him during the night until he thought he might go mad with wanting her.

Those tormenting thoughts had prompted his occasional casual mention of her to Ryker. Although Jackson would like to use the excuse that it was natural for personal feelings to spill out when two friends decompressed after a life-and-death assignment, he was realistic enough to admit he had never dealt with Claire walking away. Hadn't wanted to. *Still* didn't want to. Knowing she'd moved on, was planning to marry a man who could give her the life he never could, had been sufficient reason to stay away.

But Ryker had put Claire's life on the line, which left *him* no choice but to face her. And the emotions he'd refused to deal with. Head-on.

He scrubbed a hand over his stubbled jaw. "It'd be best if I lay out what happened from the beginning."

"Fine." Claire rose sharply. "You talk, I'll listen."

He watched as she tugged open a door on the pine armoire. She wore a soft denim shirt tied at the waist and slim jeans that molded tightly to her hips and legs. He knew what it felt like to have those legs part for him, wrap around him.

Two years of missing her, of wanting her with him, hit him like a ton of bricks.

Get a grip. He fought to repress the hungry, possessive storm inside him while watching her retrieve a rag and a bottle of cleaning solvent. Knowing he would waste his breath, he bit back the urge to suggest she wait until she felt steadier to clean up the dusting of fingerprint powder the cops had left on numerous items. Whenever she got nervous or upset, Claire was on the move. The night she'd told him goodbye, her pacing had almost worn a path in the carpet of their Cairo hotel room.

He retrieved the mop out of the bucket he'd filled with water and pine-scented disinfectant, then went to work on the bloodstain.

"A little over a month ago," he began, "terrorists kidnapped an American attaché in Singapore. We got intel he was being held in a warehouse, so Ryker and I set up surveillance until a team from our Mobile Security Division—the equivalent of SWAT—arrived. MSD went in first, then Ryker and myself. Or so I thought until I hit the doorway and realized he'd hung back. A second later, the warehouse exploded."

"The gash over your eye." Claire looked up from the brass candlestick she'd plucked off a shelf. "Is that how you got hurt?"

"Yeah, shrapnel clipped me at the same time the blast blew me out of the doorway." Jackson put his back into the mop as dark anger brewed in his gut. "The attaché and all members of the MSD team died. Turned out the terrorists weren't inside the warehouse—they detonated the blast by remote."

"Ryker?"

"Didn't hang around to check on his pals."

"And you think, because he held back, he knew the warehouse was going to explode?"

"He and I have gone through a lot of doors together over the years. He'd never hesitated until Singapore. In the split second before the blast, I saw it in his eyes—he *knew* the place was about to go up."

Claire set the candlestick she'd dusted aside, then went to work on a cobalt vase. "What happened after that?"

"I woke up in the ER, got my boss on the phone and told him I suspected Ryker had sold us out. He's like every other DSS agent, has connections all over the world, so it was anyone's guess where he'd go."

Just thinking about what Ryker had done—what he *intended* to do—filled Jackson with a rage so strong he wanted to slam his fist through a wall.

"I remembered Ryker mentioned a place he used as an off-the-book safe house in Kuala Lumpur," Jackson continued. "Getting from Singapore to Malaysia only takes a couple of hours, so the house was worth checking. Another MSD team got there just as dusk fell. When they burst in, a shadow dashed from around a corner, and they opened fire."

Jackson's insides bunched. If he'd known who the MSD team would find there, he wouldn't have told his boss about the damn safe house, just gone there on his own and dealt with Ryker. But he'd had no way of knowing.

"Was Ryker in the house?"

"No, but his wife and daughter were."

The rag in Claire's hand went still against the deep-blue vase. "You wouldn't take me into Malaysia because it was so dangerous for Americans. Especially women."

"Still is. Which is why the MSD team had no expectation an agent would risk his family that way."

The thick-planked floor now clean of blood, Jackson replaced the mop in the bucket. Next on his agenda was the building's security. He'd already arranged with Liz Scott to have OCPD do hourly patrols, but that was just the beginning of what needed to be done.

"Why was Ryker's family at the safe house?" Claire asked.

"Emily, his daughter, was ill." Jackson moved to the shop's expansive front window. It was mullioned with large diamond-shaped panes. The panes wouldn't open, which was good, but someone armed with a glasscutter and pry bar could make a silent entry in seconds. *Shatter sensors,* he determined, before looking back at Claire.

"From paperwork at the safe house we found out Emily had contracted a fever that did major damage to her heart."

He turned his attention to the shop's front door. After studying the dead bolt, he sized up the alarm panel, then the door mat. He added additional security devices for all to the mental list he was compiling. "Her only hope of survival was a transplant."

"Transplants are performed in every state. Why did Ryker risk taking his wife and sick daughter overseas?"

"Emily had a rare blood type which narrowed the chance of finding a heart through legal channels almost to zero. I figure Ryker thought his only hope of saving his child was to buy a heart on the black market. The paperwork steered us to a Malaysian surgeon known to have ties to al Qaeda. He wouldn't answer questions, but the theory is the black-market heart and surgery would have cost more than a million dollars. Which explains why Ryker sold out."

Jackson felt his anger growing, a vicious heat that would bubble in his blood if he allowed it to. "Later, we found out Ryker had been selling blank U.S. passports to a terrorist named Hassan Kaddur. After an expert forger gets through with the blanks, it'll be almost impossible to tell a fake from the real thing. That compromises unknown numbers of Americans on their own turf."

Claire placed the vase in a display cabinet near a collection of salt cellars, then turned. "None of that explains why Ryker wants to kill me."

"No, it doesn't."

Jackson moved to the cabinet where she stood. He recognized the Chanel scent that pulsed off her in little waves and made his juices swim. Years of practice had taught him how to present a certain face and attitude to the world no matter how he was feeling. It was an ability he would put to good use as long as he stayed here.

"Last night I got a call from an informant in Hong Kong. Guy named Kim. He said that the night before he'd been at an outdoor market and spotted a man built like Ryker talking on a cell phone. His hair was black instead of blond and he wore thick, horn-rimmed glasses, so Kim didn't think it was Ryker. But Kim's always looking to buy and sell intel, so he eavesdropped on the call. When Kim heard the man's voice, he was even more convinced the guy wasn't Ryker."

"But you think it was?"

"I know it was."

"So, why aren't you in Hong Kong instead of here?"

"Because Kim overheard the man say *Claire* and *Oklahoma City*. Ryker was talking about you."

Watching her, Jackson saw her breathing turn fast and shallow. Knowing the blame for her fear lay on his shoulders tore him apart. It was all he could do not to pull her against him. Hold her. Comfort her.

"This is crazy," she rasped, her fingers clenching the dust rag. "Why would Ryker come after me?"

"To get back at me. I'm the only person Ryker told about the safe house. So when the MSD team showed up there, he knew I'd survived the warehouse blast and sent SWAT to hit the house. In Ryker's mind, I'm the reason his wife and daughter are dead. His coming after you is his way of leveling the playing field."

"How?" Claire asked, staring up at him in confusion. "You and I haven't seen each other in two years. We haven't even talked. We've both moved on. Why would Ryker think he can get back at you through me?"

Jackson kept his gaze locked with hers. The huge flaw in Claire's reasoning was her assumption they'd both moved on. Only she could claim that. He had given it his best shot, but it hadn't worked. All he'd managed to do was stay away from her.

"When you spend hours on a stakeout, you have to talk about something. Ryker's pet topic was his wife and Emily. When you and I were together, your name naturally came up. Ryker knows I haven't been involved with anyone serious since you. He blames me for the death of his family and wants to even the score."

"His family," Claire repeated, her face taut with worry. "You lost your parents years ago, but what about Garrett? He's your *twin,* Jackson. You should be wherever he is, making sure Ryker doesn't get to him."

In a wave, the still-raw grief Jackson had fought hard to hold at bay washed over him. "Garrett's dead."

Her face went white and stiff. "When? How?"

"A little more than two weeks ago. He was in a Barcelona restaurant when a bomb planted there in a backpack exploded."

"Oh, God." What Jackson had said was terrible enough, but hearing it recited in a flat, empty voice iced Claire's blood. Whatever grief, whatever anger he felt was masked by a calm, unapproachable expression. But she knew he had loved his twin brother deeply, and the pain he felt must be brutal.

Pure reflex had her dropping the cleaning rag and stepping toward him. She felt Jackson's pain as if it were her own. She settled her hand on his forearm and murmured, "I'm so sorry." Beneath her palm she felt his heat, his hard-muscled strength. "I loved Garrett, too."

"Yeah." Instantly, he turned away, forcing her to drop her hand.

A dull throb settled in Claire's belly. She had turned

down his proposal and walked out on him. Why should she think he'd welcome her touch for any reason? After all, he hadn't popped back into her life for old times' sake. He was there because she was in danger. She was his current assignment.

"Do you think Ryker was behind the bombing?" she asked.

"There's no evidence to indicate that. Which doesn't mean a damn thing." He jabbed his fingers into the back pockets of his jeans. "If he was in on it and didn't want me to find out, he'd make sure he didn't leave a trail. All I know is that it's the norm for whatever group is behind a bombing to claim responsibility. That hasn't happened. But there's a terrorist cell in Barcelona controlled by Hassan Kaddur. He might have had his extremists carry out the bombing to show Ryker his thanks for funneling all those blank U.S. passports his way."

Claire picked up a brass microscope, set it back down. "So, with your family gone, you think Ryker has targeted me by default?"

"Something like that," Jackson said carefully. He could still feel the warm press of her palm against his forearm. Knowing she shared his grief—and his love for his brother—he'd been seconds from dragging her into his arms and holding her. Just holding her until the suffocating pain inside him diminished.

But if he ever had her in his arms again he wasn't sure he'd be able to let go. That complication, at least, he could avoid by keeping his hands off her.

Turning back to face her, he said, "The bottom line is

that Ryker's got you in his cross-hairs. That's why, before I caught the plane out of Barcelona, I called Tom Iverson at the Homeland Security Office here. I briefed him on Ryker and asked Tom to check on you. He came to Reunion Square this morning. The woman who owns the shop next door told him you'd gone out of town to an auction, but she didn't know where. It stood to reason Ryker wouldn't be able to find you, either, before I arrived. When I ran into you on the sidewalk and you said your handyman had been murdered, my first thought was that Ryker had shown up."

Claire's gaze dropped to the damp blotch on the floor while a sick feeling crept into her belly. "So, you think it should have been my throat that got slit, not Silas Smith's."

Jackson knew she felt guilty enough without telling her she might be right. "I changed my mind about Ryker being the killer after you and I got in here and I saw that some of the stock had been disturbed. And how Smith's throat had been cut."

"Why does that matter?"

"Ryker wouldn't have moved anything which might have tipped you that someone had broken in. He knows ten ways to kill without leaving blood you might spot. And he'd have hidden the handyman's body. You'd have seen nothing down here that would have stopped you from going upstairs where Ryker would have waited for you. Nothing."

"Could the killer have been someone he sent?" Claire asked.

"No, his wife and daughter's deaths are personal.

This is something he will deal with himself. I could be wrong, but I don't think Smith's murder has anything to do with Ryker."

"If you're right, who killed poor Silas?"

"While I'm here, I plan to try to find out." After all, keeping busy was preferable to going slowly crazy, wanting what he could no longer have.

As he'd done several times during the evening, Jackson flicked his gaze to Claire's left hand. Her *ringless* left hand. "I imagine this is going to complicate things for you, but I need to stay here until Ryker's caught. Before our search of your building I'd have suggested I bunk in the apartment across from yours where Charles lived. But since it's now a storeroom and crammed full of inventory for the shop, it looks like your couch is the only place available."

When she lifted a hand to push back her hair, Jackson noted it wasn't her usual casual gesture. It was a weary one. He heard that weariness in her voice when she said, "I want to tell you I don't need you to stay here."

"Claire—"

"I *want* to tell you that. Because your being here can't help but make things awkward between us. We didn't split up under the best of circumstances."

"Think maybe it's because only one of us wanted to part ways?" he asked neutrally.

"I couldn't stay." Her eyes remained steady on his, but her hands clenched tight. "I tried living in your world, Jackson, but it didn't work. You *know* I tried. I couldn't be what you wanted me to be."

My wife. Even after two years, he was never quite free from the drag of hurt that came when he thought about the last evening they'd spent together. He'd proposed. She'd said goodbye. End of story.

"So, I want to tell you I don't need you to stay here," she repeated, her gaze returning to the floor. "But then I picture poor Silas with his slit throat. And I think about Garrett...." Easing out a shaky breath, she remet his gaze. "I'm scared, Jackson. Terrified. I don't want to be, but I am."

"I'd wonder about you if you weren't," he said, and stopped himself before his hand lifted to stroke the dark fall of her hair. "I won't let Ryker get to you. You have my word."

"I'll hold you to that." Her smile was weak and didn't last. "So, I hope for your sake my couch doesn't have lumps."

"I bet it beats the straw mat I slept on recently in a shack in Sierra Leone," he said.

Nodding, she retrieved the rag and began wiping fingerprint powder off a leather hatbox. "I'm having a hard time accepting that all of this has happened," she said after a moment. "That I'm not going to wake up in the morning and find out it hasn't been a horrible nightmare."

Jackson wondered if she included his presence as part of that nightmare, but didn't ask. "Wish I could tell you that's all it is."

That was a lie. As grave as the situation was, he'd been looking for an excuse to see her again. Just *see* her, as if that might quell the ache of missing her that went on and on. But he hadn't made a move because he'd believed certain avenues were closed to him.

He took a step closer and breathed in a long, reckless drag of Chanel. "Claire, since you and I will be sharing space again for a time, there's a question that comes to mind."

"What?"

"I heard you were getting married." He dropped his gaze to her left hand. "And had an engagement ring with a diamond the size of a gumdrop. Just curious why you're not wearing it."

With Jackson having moved so close, Claire had to tilt her head back to meet his gaze. When she did, his spicy male scent filled her lungs, rekindling memories best left in the past.

At the moment, *he* was her greatest threat.

"Who told you I'm getting married?"

"Charles." Jackson raised a shoulder. "You remember what a soft spot I developed for the old pirate during all those times he hammered me at poker?"

"I remember."

"So, we've kept in touch. He mentions you now and then."

"Does he?" Claire kept her tone cool even as her temper built. Her surrogate grandfather had never once breathed a word about staying in contact with Jackson. And she would skin Charles McDougal alive for discussing her with the man with whom Charles *knew* she'd intentionally severed all ties.

Jackson crossed his arms over his chest. "I seem to recall Charles said your fiancé is a banker?"

"He is." She tilted her head. "Are you asking because you need to consult with a financial advisor while you're here? If so, I'm sure Brice will be happy to meet with you."

Jackson's mouth thinned. "My finances are fine. I'm just curious—if you're engaged, why you aren't wearing your ring?"

Damn you, Claire thought. Damn you for showing up when she'd spent weeks growing more and more uncertain that marrying Brice Harrison was the right thing for her to do. She'd never had to wonder about the origin of all her uncertainty, not with her system churning with so many unresolved feelings for the man for whom she'd naively tossed aside everything. The man who'd expected her to ignore her ingrained need to put down roots, to make a home, in order to wander the face of the earth forever with him. The man who hadn't offered to make any adjustments or sacrifices for her.

And here he was, back in her life, poking and prodding.

Fine, she thought. All his sudden presence did was enforce her determination to overcome once and for all whatever feelings she still harbored for him. Because she knew from experience that the instant Ryker was captured, Jackson would feed his need for being on the front lines of danger by taking off for wherever on the globe the hottest trouble was brewing. Just like before.

Fueled by a mix of pride and jaw-locking anger, she tugged the heavy gold necklace from beneath her T-shirt.

"I *am* engaged." When she dangled the chain between

her thumb and finger, light shot off the four-carat diamond like the tail of a comet. "I slide my ring onto this necklace for safekeeping when I know I'll be digging through boxes of antiques at an auction."

She had no intention of telling Jackson that she had driven home from today's auction totally unsure if she would ever slip the ring back on her finger. "Any more questions?"

He waited a beat, watching her with steady blue eyes that gave nothing away. "No," he said at last. "That covers everything I need to know."

Chapter 3

"Liz called last night when she got off duty and told me about poor Silas Smith," Allie Fielding said to Claire the next morning. "It's just…horrible."

"Beyond horrible." Picturing her dead handyman, Claire suppressed a shudder while lighting one of the many scented votive candles she habitually kept scattered throughout the shop. Slipping her lighter into the pocket of her slacks, she made a final check to ensure last night's cleaning marathon had eliminated all sign of the murder and police investigation.

Satisfied it had, she looked across the sea of lace-draped tables, curio cabinets and displays toward the main counter where her friend was disengaging two coffee cups wrapped with grippers from a cardboard carrier. A half hour remained before the shop opened, and Claire was glad for the time to spend with one of her two closest friends.

"Al, every time I closed my eyes last night, I saw Silas. Dead. Bloody."

"Hey, I wasn't even *here* and what Liz told me gave me creepy dreams. That's why I showed up bearing double espresso mocha lattes with whipped cream and chocolate. Who can get through a thing like this without chocolate?"

Claire couldn't help but return Allie's smile. Having inherited a truckload of money when her investment banker father had passed away a decade earlier, Allie Wentworth Fielding was forever changing her appearance. Today, her blond hair was a tumble of soft curls. Muted gray shadow shaded her wide-set blue eyes. A Prada suit in traffic-stopping red, its skirt slit halfway up one thigh, hugged her petite frame. Her stiletto heels matched her suit. Business sexy. A perfect look for the owner of Silk & Secrets, the shop next door that specialized in sensuous lingerie.

As Claire wound her way to the counter, a look of concern settled in Allie's eyes. "It makes my skin crawl to think about what might have happened if the killer had still been here when you got home."

"Believe me, I've thought of that, too." Claire slid onto the long-legged stool she kept near the register and took a sip of her latte. The mix of caffeine and chocolate sent a welcome kick through her system.

"Thanks, Al, this is just what I need."

"Supplying a little comfort is the least I can do." Allie rested her forearms on the counter. "Liz asked if I'd seen anyone hanging around yesterday while you were gone to that auction. I told her about a man who came into my shop, wanting to know why yours was closed. And where you were. After I described him, Liz said he works for Homeland Security."

Jackson's contact, Tom Iverson, Claire thought. "He does."

The concern in her eyes deepening, Allie regarded Claire over the rim of her coffee cup. "Liz said she couldn't go into detail, but there might be some rogue government agent out to get you. She knows that because a certain other government agent—whose picture the three of us once burned in effigy—showed up on your doorstep." As if she could peer through the ceiling into Claire's apartment, Allie shot a speculative look upward. "So, is America's answer to James Bond still here?"

"Yes." Claire fought to block the memory of the glimpse she'd gotten of Jackson around dawn when she'd tiptoed to her kitchen to grab some aspirin. He'd been asleep on her couch, his broad, tanned chest darkened by sleek black hair, a sheet barely covering his waist and below. She didn't have to wonder what he looked like beneath the sheet. She knew.

He's your past, she reminded herself, squaring her shoulders. Not your present. Certainly not your future. "Jackson may be here awhile," she added.

"And he showed up to nab the rogue agent? To keep said rogue from getting his hands on you?"

"Yes, to both."

Allie tapped blood-red manicured nails against the glass-topped counter. "I'm sending up thankful prayers that he's here to protect you. But I'm going on record to say the timing for all this sucks. Here you are in the middle of deciding whether to go through with your wedding and *he* shows up."

"I can't go through with it," Claire blurted. "I tossed and turned all last night, and right before the alarm went off I knew…." She jabbed fingers through her hair. "God, I have to talk to Brice. I have to tell him."

"Oh, sweetie." Allie gripped Claire's hand. "I know you're hurting. But with all the doubts you've been having, it would be a mistake to go through with the wedding."

Nodding, Claire gave Allie's fingers a squeeze. One of the best things about having close girlfriends was knowing you could count on their support. Claire had met Allie when she'd moved back to Oklahoma City after ending her disastrous fling with Jackson. Allie had opened her shop on the day Claire finalized her purchase of Home Treasures. They'd first met Liz that same night when she had nearly hauled them in from their sidewalk champagne celebration after they'd tipsily attempted a ceremonial burning of Jackson's photo.

After hearing Claire's tale of love gone bad, Liz torched the picture herself. Since then, the friendship between the three had flourished.

Allie knocked back the last of her latte. "From my experience, the only way to get through all this is to load the freezer with ice cream. What flavors do you want?"

"I'm a rocky road man myself," a deep voice stated.

Claire jerked her head toward the end of the counter where Jackson now stood. Dressed in a faded denim shirt and well-worn khaki pants, he had a finger looped through the handle of one of her thick ceramic mugs. His mouth was curved in a half smile.

Claire knew he made a habit of wearing soft-soled shoes and kept his pockets empty of coins and keys. No scuffs. No jingles. He moved so stealthily she hadn't even heard him walking around upstairs.

Or down the stairs at the rear of the shop.

She studied his benign expression, wondering how much of her and Allie's conversation he'd heard.

As always, he looked good. His black, shaggy hair was damp and finger-combed back, exposing the contours of his face in bold, unrelieved strokes. The gash over his left eye just added to his rakish appeal.

Claire felt the age-old pull, as sensual as a touch. She curled her nails into her palms against the memory of how it felt to have him on top of her. Bare sweat-slicked skin to bare sweat-slicked skin. She could almost feel the press of his weight, the slide of his hair-roughened leg along her smooth calf. Oh, mercy.

She blocked off the memory with its accompanying sensory illusion of mingled scents of heat and hardness and musky desire. Her insides felt as if they were on fire. *You're still officially engaged. You're not supposed to have carnal thoughts about another man.*

Thoughts that threatened the wall she'd built against Jackson Castle, stone by stone, around her heart.

He cocked his head. "You going to introduce me?"

"Of course. Allie Fielding, this is Jackson Castle." Claire gave silent thanks that her voice sounded halfway normal.

"Pleased to meet you," Jackson said.

"Same here." Pursing her mouth, Allie studied him with open intensity. "Welcome to Oklahoma City, Mr. Castle."

"Jackson."

"Jackson." The clock the size of a full moon bonged from its spot on the wall over the cash register. Allie tossed her cup and the cardboard carrier into the trash can behind the counter. "I hate to run, but I need to get my shop ready to open."

"Which one's yours?"

"Silk & Secrets." Allie sent Jackson a demure smile. "It's right next door. Stop by and look around if you have time."

"I'm not in the market for women's lingerie at the moment."

"Oh, Silk & Secrets carries more than just lingerie. I stock all sorts of sensual and erotic items. I'm sure you could find something intriguing."

After unlocking the shop's front door, Allie paused, her gaze on Jackson's. "You take good care of my friend, okay?"

"You have my word."

Sipping his coffee, Jackson watched the blonde sashay past the front window on ice-pick heels. She was a looker, but he much preferred Claire's crisp white shirt and black trousers to the flashy red suit. Then there was Claire's dark, silky hair and expressive eyes. Nothing flamboyant, but way sexy.

"Sensual and erotic items," he murmured. He had a

memory of Claire wearing the skimpy piece of black silk he'd bought for her in Belgium. Remembered the fire that burned inside him as he flicked open the two snaps at the crotch to get to her.

His finger tightened on the mug's handle. He'd over-heard enough of the women's conversation to know Claire had decided to call off her wedding. Or was it just a postponement?

Since he couldn't ask her, he would revert to his tried-and-true method of obtaining information: wait and watch.

Noting Claire's cheeks were pale with fatigue, he shifted his thoughts to practical matters.

"Get any sleep?" he asked.

"Maybe an hour, total." She pushed aside her coffee cup. "How about you?"

"Some."

"Last night you said you're staying here until Ryker's caught."

He nodded. "Or winds up dead."

"I've been wondering how you plan to spend your time while you're here?" She swung her arm in a wide arc. "I mean, you can't just stand around my shop."

In truth, he wouldn't mind hanging around the cozy shop that smelled of apples and pine while he spent his time looking at her. Just looking. And remembering.

An instant wave of frustration had him raking a hand through his still-damp hair. What the hell good would re-membering do when eventually he'd have to move on? He always moved on. And there was no way Claire would ever again go with him.

He gestured toward the front window. "The tall building across the square—when I was here before, it was vacant. For sale. What is it now?"

"The Montgomery," Claire answered. "It's been converted into upscale lofts and studio apartments, with retail on the ground floor. That's where Liz…Sergeant Scott lives."

"It's about ten stories," Jackson estimated.

"Exactly. Liz has a loft on the top floor."

"If I were Ryker, the first thing I'd do is find somewhere I could set up to watch this place. The roof or an upper window in the Montgomery might fit the bill." Jackson made a mental note to contact Liz Scott to arrange for access to the building's upper floors and roof.

"If the Montgomery didn't suit my needs," he continued, "I'd use a nondescript car with darkened windows and park in various locations around the square. Or maybe I'd get my hands on a van with a magnetic sign on the side indicating some kind of delivery service."

Feeling both cold and numb, Claire stared out the window. "Ryker wants to get back at you by killing me. Why wouldn't he just take a rifle with a scope up to the roof of the Montgomery and shoot me?"

The hand Jackson rested against the counter fisted. "To get back at me, he'll want to get up close and personal with you."

"Well." Claire tried to force back the fear that crept around her like an icy vapor. "The good news is I don't have to worry about Ryker taking pot shots at me from a distance. Talk about bad for business."

Jackson's mouth tightened. "You shouldn't have to sit in your own shop trying to make light conversation about getting killed. Because of me."

His voice was so angry, his shoulders so stiff, that Claire waited for the storm. When it didn't come, she slicked her tongue over her dry lips. "What happened isn't your fault. It's Ryker's."

She saw Jackson's face darken, a subtle change of expression. "Doesn't matter whose fault it was, he's not going to get close to you," he said flatly. "You have my word. And while it might appear that I'm just standing around, drinking coffee, what I'll be doing is reinforcing this place with surveillance equipment on loan from Homeland Security. I called Tom Iverson before I came downstairs to let him know what equipment I need. He'll deliver it this morning. I'll also be outside now and then, watching and waiting like I did late last night."

She blinked. "You went outside after we finished cleaning?"

"That's right."

"It must have been three o'clock in the morning. What were you watching?"

"Everything."

"Meaning, watching and waiting in case Ryker showed up?"

Jackson felt a muscle working in his jaw. While partners, he and Ryker had perfected the art of patience, their stillness like that of a predator waiting for its next meal. Now, they were hunting each other.

"Ryker's at the top of my list," he said. "The thing is, he

and I both know how to do surveillance without giving ourselves away. So I doubt it was him I heard across the square."

"You saw someone?"

"I *felt* someone. Then I heard him move. By the time I made my way to the other side of the square, he was gone."

Her blood running cold, Claire took a slow sip of her latte. "Could the person you heard have been whoever murdered Silas?"

"Anything's possible."

"If it was the killer, why would he risk coming back?"

"Good question. Seems to me there'd have to be something inside this building he wants. It's no doubt the reason he came here in the first place. But Smith showing up interrupted him."

Jackson glanced around the shop at what he considered an amazing array of merchandise. There were delicate figurines, bottles of varying sizes and colors. Teapots, china, pillows, laces and shawls. Trays of brass, pewter and gleaming copper. As he had the first time he walked into Home Treasures, he wondered why anyone would want to clutter their lives with so much stuff.

"What's in here that's so valuable?" he asked, looking back at Claire. "That's worth the killer risking coming back?"

Claire shook her head. "Nothing."

"If it was him out there early this morning, there's something." Jackson furrowed his brow. "Have you bought anything out of the ordinary? Some knickknack worth a ton of money?"

"No, nothing like that." Claire stroked her fingertips

up and down her throat. "If I've got something in here that someone wants that badly, why not just come in when the shop's open and buy it?"

"Could be it's something that's not for sale."

Jackson shifted back toward the large storefront window. Instantly, he spotted a man, tall and lean and dressed in a tailored black suit, starched white shirt and coral tie.

"Looks like you've got your first customer of the day," he said when the man strode toward the door.

Claire glanced up. Jackson saw dislike flash in her eyes before she masked it.

"Hell just froze over," she murmured, and moved around the counter as the man stepped through the door. "Mr. Navarro, welcome to Home Treasures."

"Claire. You look lovely, as always."

"Thank you."

Jackson watched the man's lips pull back to reveal a flash of white teeth. Instead of shaking the hand Claire offered, he pressed his lips against her knuckles. His dark hair and olive skin evidenced his Latino heritage, as did the light sprinkling of Hispanic accent.

"Are you here on art council business, Mr. Navarro?"

"No, I'm shopping." He glanced at Jackson. "But I see you already have a customer. I'll browse until you're finished helping this gentleman."

"I'm not a customer." Stepping forward, Jackson offered his hand, forcing the man to release his hold on Claire. "Jackson Castle."

"Adam Navarro." He raised a dark eyebrow. "Do you live in Oklahoma City, Mr. Castle?"

"No, I'm in town on business."

"Business?"

Nosy bastard. "I'm a geologist." It was a cover Jackson often used since both his parents and twin brother had been geologists and he knew the lingo.

"Ah," Navarro said. "We have enough oil and gas in Oklahoma to keep any number of geologists busy."

"That's a fact," Jackson agreed. Curious over Claire's comment about hell freezing over, he lingered at the counter. "And your business is?"

"I'm curator of the National Cowboy and Western Heritage Museum. People travel from all over the world to visit us. If you haven't been to the museum, I urge you to come."

"Actually, I stopped by your museum when I was here a couple of years ago." Jackson slid a look at Claire and felt dark satisfaction when he saw the blush that had risen in her cheeks.

Clearly, she remembered the summer afternoon they had spent at the museum. At one point they'd found it impossible to keep their hands off each other and had wound up in a dark alcove. He would have done a lot more than kiss her blind if the small cubicle had had a damn door.

"I have fond memories of your museum, Mr. Navarro," he added mildly.

"Wonderful."

Claire kept her attention focused on her customer. "So, you said you're here to shop?"

"Yes. I had lunch the other day with your future mother-in-law. I mentioned to Virginia that my sister is looking for old leather-bound books to use as decor in the shop she's opening in Dallas. A children's clothing and furniture store. Virginia said you maintain a good supply of leather-bound books."

"That's right. People are always wanting them for decor in offices and studies. Even nurseries."

"Excellent. My sister has her heart set on using only children's books."

Jackson watched them move toward a corner of the shop fashioned into a study with several bookcases and a throne-like chair that looked as if it belonged in some English castle. Navarro paused before one of the bookshelves, running his fingertips across a row of leatherbound spines. His gold cuff link glinted with the gesture.

Jackson looked back toward the window. His narrowed gaze tracked a white van pulling to a stop. A sign on the van identified it as a florist delivery truck. *Maybe,* Jackson thought. *Maybe not.*

He watched the driver slide out the door, then move to the rear of the van where he retrieved a vase holding an explosion of yellow roses. The man was shorter than Ryker. Didn't mean Ryker hadn't hired the guy to check out the shop.

And Claire.

"These are for Claire Munroe," the driver said when Jackson met him outside the door.

"I'll see she gets them." Jackson traded the bills he dug out of his pocket for the flowers. "Thanks."

"Sure." If the driver's goal had been to get a look at Claire, he'd failed.

By the time Jackson had settled the vase on the counter, Claire and Navarro were back. When she spotted the roses, a crease formed between her brows.

"These books are perfect," Navarro commented. "I only wish you had double the number."

"I do have one more," she said. "But its cover is damaged so I plan to have it repaired before I place it in stock."

Navarro nodded. "Why don't you let me take a look at it? My sister's shop has a large number of nooks and crannies to fill. One book with a damaged cover can be easily camouflaged."

"It's upstairs in my apartment. It will only take me a minute to get it."

"I'm in no hurry."

As Claire headed toward the rear of the shop, Navarro leaned in to sniff the roses. "I don't have to wonder who these are from."

Jackson sipped his coffee. "That a fact?"

"Brice Harrison has reserved one of the event rooms at the museum for his and Claire's wedding reception. The florist has been by twice to measure space for urns that will be filled with yellow roses."

Like any cop, Jackson never let an opportunity to obtain information pass by. "I haven't met Harrison yet. What does he do for a living?"

"He's vice president of the city's largest bank. And he sits on the museum's board of directors."

"Meaning, he's one of your bosses?"

"Correct."

"Here it is," Claire said. The book in her hands was

dusty, the edges worn. She flipped through the pages, pulled out a thin piece of paper and laid it aside on the counter. "I try to go through all the books and pull out the little scraps and whatnot people use for bookmarks." She handed the book to Navarro. "You may change your mind about buying it, now that you see how loose the binding is."

"It's fine. My sister can have it repaired if she chooses."

"All right, but I'm reducing the price due to the damage."

Smiling, Navarro handed her a credit card. "I see you know how to instill satisfaction in your customers, Claire."

"That's my goal."

Just then, Jackson's cell phone rang. Pulling it from his pocket, he answered the call on his way out the shop's front door. He listened while a fellow agent detailed the latest locations where personnel had been dispatched to hunt for Ryker. And frowned over the news that the rogue agent had yet to be spotted.

When Navarro stepped from the shop with his purchases, Jackson returned the curator's brisk nod.

A moment later, he ended the call. Instead of returning to the shop, Jackson turned toward the window and watched Claire.

She stood at the counter, the small card that had come with the flowers clenched in one hand. After a moment, she picked up the phone and dialed. Then she closed her eyes while sadness clouded her face like a veil.

Not her finest moment, Claire thought hours later.

Standing at the waist-high railing that rimmed her

building's rooftop terrace, she gazed down at Reunion
Square. The moonlight painted the darkened shops and
apartment building across the way in subdued shades of
gray and black, with occasional patches of white. The air
was a warm caress against the flesh not covered by the
sundress she'd changed into before Brice arrived. The
wine she sipped was a cool salve against the rawness in
her throat.

Rawness brought on by regret at the hurt she had seen
in Brice's eyes when she'd returned his engagement ring
and called off their wedding. He'd stood in the center of
her living room, his eyes solemn. *I love you, Claire. But
I don't want to be someone you settle for.*

She dragged in a ragged breath. Most women would
have been happy to "settle" for the life Brice Harrison
could give them. A vice president of a bank, he owned a
spacious home in the city's most elite suburb. He was a
gorgeous, honorable man who wanted to give Claire
From-the-Wrong-Side-of-the-Tracks Munroe everything
she'd dreamed of.

There had to be something screwy coded into her
DNA, she decided while downing a healthy swallow of
wine. Once upon a time she'd actually found Mr. Right,
but he'd had the wrong lifestyle. Time passed, and she
found the right lifestyle, but Mr. Wrong was living it.

The stars that flamed like torches against the navy-
blue sky blurred against a swell of tears. Jackson resur-
facing in her life just when she'd decided to call off her
wedding was in-your-face proof she was incapable of
having it all.

"Damn screwy DNA," she muttered.

"Claire?"

Her shoulders tightened at the sound of Jackson's voice coming from behind her. Naturally, she hadn't heard him approach.

At least he'd asked no questions when she'd told him she was having company that evening and wanted privacy. He'd faded into the storage room across the hall from her apartment to finish setting up the monitors and running diagnostics on the equipment he'd borrowed from Homeland Security. But now that Brice was gone, it was time for Jackson to reappear out of the shadows. Literally.

"Nice night," he said, stepping to the railing.

"Yes."

"Mind if I ask you a question?"

She slid him a look. If he expected her to discuss Brice, he was nuts. "Yes, I mind. It's not something I want to talk about."

"If that's the case, you shouldn't have mentioned it in the first place."

Brow furrowed, she sipped her wine while studying him. The man had always looked magnificent in the moonlight. Bold, exciting, dangerous. Nothing had changed. *Dammit.*

"Mentioned what?"

"Right before Adam Navarro walked into the shop this morning, you said that hell was about to freeze over. And if I read you right, he's not your favorite person. Why?"

"Oh." She attempted to roll some of the tension from her shoulders. The museum curator was a safe topic. "I

mentioned hell because when Charles owned Home Treasures, the last thing Navarro would have done is darken
the shop's threshold."

"Why?"

"I'm not sure what happened that first made Charles
and Navarro lock horns, but there's always been a professional rivalry between them. Things only got worse
when Navarro told Charles during a function at the
museum that he viewed an antique dealer like Charles as
little better than a flea-market peddler."

"Sort of the equivalent of Michelangelo looking down
his nose at a common house painter?" Jackson asked
with a grin.

"Exactly. From what I understand, the discussion got
heated and after that their feud turned personal. Very
personal. Suffice it to say Navarro would have choked
today if he'd known the children's books he bought were
part of a shipment of items Charles purchased at a recent
estate sale."

"Is their personal feud the reason you don't like
Navarro?"

"Mainly. On a professional level, there's been gossip that
he's bypassed steps required in authenticating certain items
obtained for the museum. Nothing's ever been proven."

"Interesting."

Beside her, Jackson shifted and glanced across his
shoulder. Claire could almost feel his mind cataloguing
the patio chairs and small wrought-iron tables she'd
placed on a bright all-weather area rug. She'd outlined
the courtyard she'd created with pots brimming with

flowers that burst in wild, careless color and filled the air with perfume and promise.

"You've made yourself a nice place up here," he said, looking back at her. "It reminds me of that rooftop restaurant in Paris. We danced until closing time. Remember?"

She took a bracing breath. She remembered everything about that night. The torchy tunes that swirled in the warm Paris air. The heady taste of champagne. The feel of Jackson's arms around her. The press of his body against hers that was like a flame against a river of oil. Yes, she'd envisioned that rooftop setting when she created this one.

But too much time had passed for her still to be seduced by those memories. She could now appreciate the night for what it was, and not spin dreams around it she knew could never come true.

"How about we don't talk about our past?"

"Fine, let's talk about the present. You've had a rough time of things and it seems to me you could use a friend."

She regarded him over the rim of her glass. "Finding Silas Smith murdered, and learning your former partner wants to kill me because of our relationship that ended two years ago feels a little more than 'rough.'"

"I'm not talking about Smith or Ryker." Settling a hand on her arm, Jackson nudged her around to face him. His warm, calloused palm pressed against her flesh, stirring hot, bittersweet memories. As did the eyes that stared down at her, glinting with blue intensity in the moonlight.

"I overheard your conversation this morning with Allie. About you calling off your wedding. Then you received enough roses to fill a greenhouse. You told me you wanted privacy tonight because you were expecting a visitor. A man showed up and stayed less than an hour. He didn't look happy when he left. Now, you're standing on a dark roof, with misery in your eyes."

She could deny it, but what was the use? "You haven't lost your keen observation skills, Special Agent Castle. I'm no longer engaged."

"Whatever your reasons, it has to be painful."

"True, which is why I don't want to talk about it."

"We don't have to talk." Jackson's thumb caressed her flesh, as light as a breeze, yet stirring sensations deeper than a storm.

He leaned in, blocking out the moonlight, the night. "We weren't just lovers, Claire. We were friends. A lot has changed, but I'd like to think that hasn't. If you need a shoulder to lean on, I've got two available."

In those crazy, heady months they'd spent together, she'd found she could talk to him about anything. They'd laughed, shared private jokes. Both had reveled in just being together during chunks of time they managed to steal between Jackson's assignments.

It had always been that way with them, so relaxed, so comfortable.

A weight settled over her, as dark as the night. The last thing she felt now was relaxed. Comfortable. Not with Jackson standing so close she could see the rough shadow of beard that darkened his cheeks and jaw. Just remembering the erotic scrape of his jaw against her skin was enough to make her go weak at the knees.

"I'll keep your offer in mind." When she started to shift away, he didn't immediately release his hold on her. Instead, his hand slid down her arm, her wrist, his fingers brushing the slope of her palm. Her hand tingled.

Stepping away, she raised her glass to her lips. She didn't know how to fight her body's reaction to him, but she did know she wasn't going to wind up in his arms. Not when she felt so vulnerable. Unsettled. Not while her pulse jumped and her skin shivered from the heat of his nearness.

Not when she'd learned the hard way that she would always come in a distant second to his job.

It would help, she decided, to think of Jackson Castle as a shadow from her past come back to haunt her. One that would eventually disappear from her life. Nothing more.

"Like you said, I've had a rough time of it. I'm going to bed." She offered him her wine. "Goodnight, Jackson."

He took the glass, his fingers skimming a caress over hers that spiked her already hammering pulse.

"Goodnight."

With his lungs filled with the soft scent of Chanel, he watched her turn. The back of her dress was cut low; as she walked, the mossy-green material poured over her figure like a second skin. He knew beneath the dress her hips were the color of slivered almonds, her belly smooth and gently rounded. Her breasts were high and shapely. He remembered every curve, every dip. Remembered just where to touch to have her moaning and trembling beneath him.

His blood heated as he tracked her across the shadowy rooftop to the stairs. Then she was gone.

He closed his eyes. His chest felt as if someone had kicked it. Nearly three years ago, he'd walked into Home Treasures for the first time and she'd smiled up at him from behind the counter. From that moment, he'd wanted her more than he had ever wanted anything—or anyone—in his life.

Nothing had changed.

It was as plain and simple as that. Only things weren't at all plain. And their relationship had been anything but simple.

He couldn't stay in one place with her and still do the job that was a part of who he was; she couldn't live a rootless existence with him.

"Dammit to hell." Jackson angled the glass toward the moonlight, saw the lipstick kiss Claire's mouth had left on its rim. Pressing his lips over the kiss, he drained the wine and barely prevented himself from heaving the glass against the building's ledge.

Nothing had changed.

Nothing would ever change.

Chapter 4

"How can anyone live around all this clutter?" Jackson asked two days later as he stood in the doorway of a bedroom in a house that smelled of dank air and mothballs.

"Not clutter, treasures." Clicking on the camera feature of her cell phone, Claire snapped a picture of the iron bedstead propped against the room's far wall. "I imagine the elderly owners of this place wish they could move their belongings with them into the retirement center."

Jackson regarded the matching bureaus and nightstands, their tops covered with ivory-colored doilies and glass figurines. The downstairs rooms were in the same state—brimming with antique furniture and knickknacks. Every inch of the hardwood floors were covered with rugs. There were so many hanging plates, trays and pictures that it was impossible to distinguish the pattern of the wallpaper. In the dining room, he had envisioned the massive table and breakfront groaning from the weight of the silver platters and stacks of china painted with tiny flowers.

Which, he noted, were the type of dishes Claire mostly owned. The kind that people passed to the next generation. His own mother had opted for thick ceramic dishes that could withstand the constant moves his geologist parents made over the years.

With a career that had so far landed him on every continent except Antarctica, Jackson didn't even own dishes. He just used the ones that came with the furnished D.C. condo he rented. And rarely inhabited.

He watched Claire ease past a rocking chair, then a table piled with linens to look at the price tag dangling from the iron headboard.

"You thinking of buying that?" he asked.

"Not for myself." Her thumb danced across the buttons of her phone. "Liz—Detective Scott—is getting married in a couple of months. She's got her heart set on an antique iron bedstead, and asked me to keep an eye open for one. I just sent her the picture and price."

"Thing must weigh a ton. She'll have fun hauling it up to her loft at the Montgomery."

"I know a couple of hulking guys who own a moving company." After slipping her phone back into her purse, Claire ran a hand over the headboard. "Liz will love this."

The sheer lust that whipped through Jackson while he watched Claire caught him off guard. He didn't have to imagine what it would be like to wrap her fingers around those iron posts, hold them there while he thrust into her. He had done just that in a similar bed they'd shared in Marrakesh. Even after a space of two years he could see her dark hair spilling across the pillow, the flutter of her lashes in the candlelight, her brownish-gold eyes turning smoky with desire.

For him. Then, he'd been all she wanted. She was still the only woman he wanted.

With his blood running hot, fast and greedy, his gaze slid down her long, supple length. Dressed in slim coral slacks and a sleeveless white top which left her tanned shoulders and lightly muscled arms bare, she looked all tidy and crisp. Calm and cool.

Which is how she had acted toward him during the past two days. Calm and cool and distantly polite. Meanwhile, his constant awareness of her kept him on edge. Unsettled. And during the nights, while he lay on the couch picturing her in bed just one room away, his blood raced so hot he was surprised steam didn't rise through his pores.

Taking a deep breath, he reminded himself of why he was camped on her couch at night and spending his days monitoring the surveillance equipment on loan from Homeland Security.

Frank Ryker.

Jackson had lost count of the number of calls he'd made to his contacts around the world, hoping to pick up the rogue agent's scent. So far, nothing.

Thinking about Ryker had anger clawing through Jackson while a dark inevitability settled around him.

His gut told him his former mentor and partner had orchestrated the bombing that killed his twin brother. Then there was the conversation in Singapore that Jackson's snitch had overheard, during which Claire's name was mentioned.

He knew how Ryker operated. Knew how his mind worked. Jackson didn't for one minute believe the man who'd taught him how to move across any terrain in a way that made a chameleon look flamboyant had gone permanently underground. Not when his goal was to revenge the deaths of his wife and daughter.

Ryker was coming after Claire. What Jackson didn't know was how or when.

Still positioned in the doorway, he focused his narrowed gaze down the long, dim hallway. He listened intently until he was sure he and Claire were still the only people inside the house. The estate sale of the elderly couple's belongings didn't kick off until morning. But a pal of Claire's was running the show and had let her come by this evening to preview the merchandise.

So, here they were, Jackson thought. Claire sizing up the iron bed while he pictured her sharing it with him.

It was all he could do not to step into the bedroom, pull her into his arms, thread his hands through her thick black hair and taste her mouth.

"I'm done here." Shifting around, she met his gaze. Instantly, a look crossed her face, a quick shadow before she turned her head.

"Something wrong?"

"No." She moved to the table, thumbed through the

stack of linens while saying, "The only thing left I want to look at is the patio furniture. It's stored in the garage so we need to go out the back door."

Jackson watched her for a long moment while regret washed over him for what he hadn't been able to give her. Would never be able to give her.

He stepped back into the hallway. "After you."

By the time they walked outside into the early-evening light, Claire's teeth were clenched tight enough to crack fillings.

In the bedroom, when she'd glimpsed the hunger in Jackson's face, she had known exactly what he'd been thinking. Remembering. The iron bedstead looked so much like the one in Marrakesh that her throat had closed when she'd first spotted it. While sending Liz the photo and price of the bed, Claire had tried to suppress the memory of that scorching summer night, of her hands gripping the rungs of the headboard while Jackson moved inside her. Of her matching each slow, smooth stroke. But the memory had already planted its claws and she couldn't shake it.

Curling her fingers into fists, she crossed the flag-stone terrace in silence. Over the past forty-eight hours her life had turned upside down into something she barely recognized.

"Do you have the key?" Jackson asked when they reached the wooden garage that stood separate from the house.

Claire nodded. Standing beside her in his dark sport shirt and khaki pants, Jackson looked like a typical man who toiled in an office during the week and played golf in his off time. But his casual dress could not hide his soldier's body, tough and lean. Claire knew better than anyone what Jackson did for a living. Knew the vast amount of time and money the U.S. State Department invested in training its special agents in firearms use, evasive driving, dignitary protection, passport fraud and the hunting of fugitives on foreign soil. She knew that danger was an inherent part of the career that took Jackson from one hot spot of the globe to another.

A career he loved. One he wasn't likely ever to give up.

With a sigh, she pulled the key out of her pocket and undid the padlock. Jackson tugged open the double doors, reached in and flipped on the overhead light, then stepped back so she could enter first. She got halfway to the center of the garage when her heart surged into her throat.

She stopped so abruptly it was all Jackson could do not to plow into her from behind. In the lightbulb's dim glow, he watched the blood drain out of Claire's face. Her attention wasn't focused on the wrought-iron patio furniture grouped on one side of the cluttered garage, but on the old turquoise van that took up the other half.

He saw the hand she lifted to her throat tremble.

"Claire, what's wrong?"

"The van…."

He studied the vehicle. It was at least thirty years old, and had the dents and rust spots to prove it.

"Looks like something out of the hippie era," he said. "Did you own one like it?"

"My mother did."

The air in the garage was as still as death as Jackson waited for her to continue. The only time Claire had mentioned her mother was to tell him she'd been a teenager when the woman had died. From the look on Claire's face, whatever memories the van stirred up were wrought with emotion.

"When I was little, my mother always worked in some bar," Claire said, shoving a hand through her hair. She rarely talked about her mother, but seeing the van had memories shooting out like pebbles from a slingshot and she couldn't keep them in. "She would drop everything for a man. We'd pack up the van and move to Alaska, if that's what the current object of her desire wanted. When the relationship ended, which it always did, she would meet someone else and off we'd go again. I lost track of how many places we lived—different rent houses, different schools, different faces."

"What about your father?" Jackson asked quietly.

"Mother always said he took off the instant he found out she was pregnant. I think the truth is, she didn't know which of her lovers had planted the seed."

Claire raised a shoulder. "I loved her, but she wasn't like other mothers who drove car pools and wore jogging outfits. Mine wiggled around in tight jeans. Other mothers taught their kids not to steal. Mine convinced me it was okay to swipe salt and pepper shakers from restaurants."

"I take it you wound up in Oklahoma City because your aunt lived here?" Jackson asked.

"Yes. We moved here after one of Mother's breakups turned exceptionally nasty. That's when she started drinking heavily. She lost job after job, and sometimes didn't have enough money to buy food, much less pay the rent. By the time I was ten, we were living out of the back of our van. It was summer, and stifling. When my aunt found out, she offered to let us move in with her. Mother had too much pride to accept. But she knew I wanted to go with my aunt, so she let me."

"Did your aunt already live in the apartment you do now?"

"She had just moved in there. Charles and his wife lived across the hall, and they took both of us under their wings. For the first time I knew what it was like to have a real family."

"How often did you see your mother after that?"

"Off and on." Claire tried to mask it, but was aware of the splinter of pain that crept into her voice. "When I was seventeen, she drank herself to death."

She stared at the vehicle, acknowledging that the raging, tearing grief she'd initially felt over her mother's death had transformed over time into a phantom ache. "It seems like all that happened a lifetime ago," she added.

"I'm sorry, Claire."

At Jackson's soft murmur, she felt the sudden heat of embarrassment in her cheeks. "So am I. We came out to look at patio furniture and here I am, dumping on you about my past. Seeing that van—the exact style as the one we lived in—took me off-guard, that's all."

He turned to face her. "I'm sorry things were so bad for you growing up," he said, his gaze locked with hers. As he spoke, he slipped one hand around the back of her neck. His touch felt warm, but sent a shiver of anticipation along her nerve endings. "I wish you'd told me about your past with your mother when we were together."

When he traced his thumb along her hairline, Claire felt every atom of her skin come alive. It wasn't embarrassment heating her flesh now. It was a wave of unspeakable longing. Already he was chipping through the wall around her heart, making her remember, making her feel things she didn't want to feel.

Which was the last thing she needed with her nerves already stretched and raw.

"Why?" She lifted her chin. "Would knowing about my childhood have made a difference when you proposed? Would that have prompted you to stay in one place and make a permanent home with me?"

His expression remained neutral, but Claire could feel the emotion radiating from his hand still pressed to the back of her neck.

"I can't do my job by staying in one place," he said after a moment. "That's why I asked you to travel with me. I wanted us to be together."

"No, you wanted me to follow you around the world. Wanted me to be ready and waiting for you between assignments." She felt a wrench of regret as she took a step back, forcing him to drop his hand. "We want different things, Jackson. Different lifestyles. We'll never be anything but wrong for each other."

She glanced over her shoulder at the van. "Let's get out of here," she said, then headed for the door.

"I need to check the security equipment." With a hand on the knob of the door to the storage room, Jackson lingered across the hallway while Claire unlocked the door to her apartment.

"Take your time." Inching the door open, she met his gaze over her shoulder. His eyes held hers with the same grim assessment she'd seen during dinner, which they'd spent mostly in silence. "I'm going to pour a glass of wine and go up on the roof for a while."

"Want some company?"

"No." She clenched her fingers around her keys. When she'd spotted the van at the estate sale, it wasn't just the age-old ache she had felt over wondering if she could have changed her mother's fate if she had stayed and lived with her in the van. Claire was aware she had abandoned Jackson, too.

At the very last breath of their lives together she remembered pacing their hotel room in Cairo, gripping the jewelry box he had given her only moments before, trying to make him understand why she couldn't accept his engagement ring. Couldn't marry him. Had to leave.

She wanted a man who stayed in one place, who would share a home with her, be there to raise their children. Still, her experience with Brice Harrison was proof those things weren't enough. She wanted love, too. The passionate, soul-deep love she'd once felt for Jackson.

Her gaze drifted back across the hallway to where he

stood. What would have happened if she had stayed with him? Could they have found some way to give each other the type of life they both needed?

He'll leave, she reminded herself. Once Frank Ryker was in custody, Jackson would get a call from his boss and be off to Caracas or Moscow or Zimbabwe. Just like before.

Now, though, she had her home. Her shop. They were enough to make her happy. She would make sure they were enough.

"Thanks for the offer of company," she added. "I just… I have some thinking to do."

In the bright illumination from the hallway's antique wall sconces, the contrast between Jackson's tanned skin and his Adriatic-blue eyes was compelling. "I'll see you later, then."

"All right."

She stepped into her apartment, using her elbow to close the door behind her as she flicked on the light switch. She saw the rubble in her living room at the same time as a large hand clamped over her mouth and an arm around her waist lifted her off her feet.

Ryker! Panic screamed through her. Her purse slid off her shoulder, thudded to the floor. She heard her own muffled screams and knew the sound wouldn't carry beyond the room. She clawed at the hand over her mouth, kicking and squirming in an effort to escape.

Her assailant tightened his hold, locking her against his hard body. "Do what I say, or you're dead."

It wasn't the vicious whisper that stopped Claire's

struggling, but the prick of a blade against her throat. The image of Silas Smith careened into her brain, his neck a bloody gash as he lay dead on the floor of her shop.

A moment of sheer terror took her, making her so weak she could hardly draw breath past the gloved hand pressed against her mouth and nose. Darkness loomed at the edges of her vision, a tunnel narrowing.

"I heard you talking to the guy in the hall," the man whispered. "Sounds like he'll be in here soon, so you and I need to get our business done fast. Understand?"

She gave a jerky nod. Despite the latex covering his hand, she could smell the sour scent of his sweat, mixed with a cheap cologne that threatened to turn her stomach. Clenching her teeth, she forced herself not to gag.

He shifted her so she had a clear view of her living room; every drawer had been pulled out, its contents dumped on the floor. Her couch was turned over, the cushions slashed. The books that had filled her small antique bookcase lay in a heap.

"If you hadn't hid it so good, I'd already been gone," he whispered against her ear. "So you get to deal with me." She winced when the knife's point gouged her skin. "Like your handyman did."

The full meaning of his words clicked in her terrified brain. Icy fear bubbled up inside her, had her jerking forward.

His imprisoning grip held firm. "Stay still," he ordered while the tip of the knife pierced her flesh.

Burning pain took her breath away. She felt a warm stream of blood trickle down her neck.

"If you don't want to wind up like the old man, you'll tell me where the paper is."

Oh God. Oh God. He'd murdered Silas! And he would kill her, too, if she didn't give him the paper. *What paper?* Why would Ryker want a paper from her? Was it possible whoever held her in a death grip wasn't the rogue government agent?

She still had the building's keys gripped in her hand. In self-defense class she'd learned to use the serrated edge of a key as a weapon. Right now, though, she was shaking so hard she knew she was lucky still to have a grip on the keys.

When she didn't instantly answer, he increased the pressure on the blade. "If you don't talk, I'll make you eat this knife. Now, tell me where it is."

"Downstairs," she blurted. *Jackson.* She had to somehow alert Jackson. "It's…downstairs."

"Where?"

"Hidden." Even as her frantic mind whirled, ice-edged horror reduced her voice to a whimper. "There's…a loose…floorboard."

"Which one?"

"Near the…Dresden vases."

"I don't know what the hell those are," he hissed.

That's what she'd been counting on. "I'll…show you."

Light glinted in a shimmering arc as the knife's blade swept in front of her eyes. She saw his shirt's black sleeve; beneath the latex glove his skin looked as pale as death.

"I've given you two little nicks, sweetheart," he said, his breath a hot wash against her ear. "You make one sound, one false move when we get outside that door, I'll cut you. There's a difference between a nick and a cut. Ain't no problem to show you. Understand?"

Claire bit down on the terror. "Yes."

"Move." He replaced the blade's sharp edge against the racing pulse in her throat, then propelled her to the door. "Open it slow."

Tears stung her eyes, but she fought them back. She wasn't helpless—wouldn't be helpless. He might kill her, but she wouldn't make it easy.

She gripped the doorknob, turned it and eased the door open. Her gaze shot to the storage room across the hall. When Jackson had entered it to check the surveillance equipment, he had shut the door.

She tightened her fingers on the keys.

"Not one sound," the man hissed, then nudged her into the hallway.

With survival her only thought, Claire lobbed the keys. The same instant they clattered against the closed door, she surged up on tiptoe and slammed the back of her head against her attacker's nose.

Stars flashed before her eyes. The sick crunch of cartilage sounded in her head and she felt the reflexive loosening of his grip on her waist. The hand holding the knife jerked aside; using the force of both arms, she rammed her elbow into his stomach.

He grunted with pain as his hand slid from her mouth.

"Jackson!" she screamed at the exact moment the door to the storage room swung open.

Jackson came in low, weapon drawn.

Claire saw his eyes sweep from her to the man behind her, then to the knife in his hand.

"Toss it down," the man hissed. "I'll cut her if you don't get rid of the gun."

"Sure." With his eyes fixed on the man's, Jackson crouched, set his gun on the floor. Then he lunged.

She caught a flash of the fierceness in Jackson's eyes seconds before he delivered one chop to the man's wrist, sending the knife flying.

Jackson dragged her from the man's grip. Before he shoved her behind him, Claire glimpsed her attacker for the first time. He didn't look anything like the pictures of Ryker that Jackson had shown her. His coloring was wrong, even the shape of his face.

Jackson blocked the foot the man kicked toward his head and heaved his opponent into a backward stumble.

"Lock yourself in your apartment!" Jackson yelled, as he advanced toward the man. Instead of meeting the challenge, the intruder turned and bolted toward the stairs.

Claire kicked the knife away then swept up the gun, straightening in time to see Jackson tackle his quarry. They plunged down the staircase together in a violent tangle of limbs and curses.

A crack and the splintering of wood registered in Claire's numb brain. Gun clenched at the ready, she scrambled down the staircase, almost tumbling into the storeroom when she reached for the banister and encountered air instead.

Regaining her balance, she looked at the bottom of the stairs. She had a partial view of a man's body, lying as still as death.

Chapter 5

At the bottom of the staircase, Jackson rolled to his feet and braced for attack.

No need, he realized after one look at the man sprawled on the floor. His neck was angled so far backward there was no question the scum was dead.

"Jackson!"

He had just enough time to turn before Claire launched herself off the stairs and into his arms.

If her attacker hadn't already been dead, he'd have killed him, Jackson thought while he eased his gun from her clenched fingers. Since she'd locked onto him like a burr, he could feel her lungs heaving almost as crazily as his.

"You're bleeding." He shoved the automatic into the holster he wore at the small of his back then nudged her dark hair behind her shoulder. The trickle of blood he'd spotted on the side of her throat had now congealed, telling him the wound was superficial.

"Baby, did he cut you anywhere else?"

"No. Oh, God!"

She shifted, burrowed deeper against his shoulder. He pressed his fingertips against the uninjured side of her throat. Her pulse hammered erratically, but strong.

"I thought…it was Ryker," she whispered, her voice a bare thread of sound. "I thought it was *him*."

Jackson looked down at the dead man, examining him with a cop's eye to detail. The intruder was taller than Ryker, lankier and his skin tone was darker. "It's not Ryker." Still, Jackson knew that his traitorous ex-partner could have sent the intruder.

Easing her head back, Claire gazed up at him through glassy eyes. "When I saw you plunge down the stairs, then heard the banister snap, I thought… Jackson, are you okay?"

"I've got a couple of bruises, is all," he said, keeping his voice calm and quiet. "Looks like I owe you a new banister."

Although he'd forced his mouth to curve, inside he was as taut as a coiled spring.

None of the surveillance equipment he'd checked showed that the building's security had been breached while he and Claire were at the estate sale. He needed to find out how the bastard had got inside the building, but that could wait. Claire was his first concern. She was close to shock—he could feel it in the cold dampness of her skin, the uncontrollable shaking of her body against his.

He damned himself that the bastard had got to her. He was there to protect her, and he'd been across the hall when she needed him. He didn't want to think about what would have happened if she hadn't managed to signal him that she needed help.

"Let's get back to your apartment and call the police," he said, then lifted her into his arms.

"I was so scared, I couldn't think what to do," Claire said an hour later. With the slit cushions repositioned upside down, she huddled against one end of her couch. The comforter wrapped around her did nothing to ward off the chill in her bones. And, despite the ointment and gauze pad a paramedic had applied, the nicks on the side of her throat still stung.

"You did fine." Sitting in the center of the couch, Detective Liz Scott reached out and gripped Claire's hand. With her long coppery hair swept back into an intricate French braid, Liz's emerald-green eyes looked huge, her high cheekbones sharp. "You had the presence of mind to toss your keys against the storage-room door and alert Castle. Believe me, not every assault victim manages to think so coolly."

Claire shook her head. "I just knew if I didn't do *something,* I wasn't getting out of here alive."

Liz gave Claire's hand a squeeze before releasing it, then glanced down at her notepad. "You're sure you have no idea what paper the guy was talking about?"

"No clue."

Muted conversation, then the chirp of a cell phone

pulled Claire's gaze to the apartment's open door. Out in the hallway, Liz's tall gangly partner pulled his phone out of his black suit coat at the same time Jackson stepped into the apartment. The two men had left a half hour ago to check the building to try to ascertain the intruder's point of entry.

"I just talked to the alarm company," Jackson stated. "They verify the system was enabled until eight-seventeen. Which was the time Claire and I got back here and she entered her code."

Liz gestured toward the pile of books and rubble from the overturned drawers. "The bedroom and kitchen are in the same state, which probably took the guy at least half an hour. I figure he'd have started searching the shop next if Claire hadn't walked in on him. Did you find his point of entry?"

"The roof," Jackson answered, his grim gaze settling on Claire.

She felt the sharp assessment in his blue eyes as he replaced the upholstered cushion—slit-side down—onto the wingback chair near her end of the couch. Still lingering inside her were the remnants of the debilitating fear and icy panic that had gripped her. However, the most threatening, confusing emotions she felt at the moment concerned the man now sitting only a few feet away. She'd worked so hard to forget everything about him. But launching herself off the staircase at Jackson had brought the memories careening back…of lying in his arms, of feeling his hard body against her own, of missing him so much she thought she might die from it.

Damn Frank Ryker for targeting her for revenge, and bringing Jackson Castle back into her life.

"There's an air-conditioning vent in the stairwell to the roof," Jackson continued. "The vent cover has been pried off. That's how the bastard got in."

Claire frowned. "My building's two stories and doesn't have a fire escape, so there's no outside access to the roof. No buildings butt up to mine. How did the man get up there?"

"One of the lab techs found scuff marks near your rooftop terrace," Jackson explained. "Another tech checked the roof of the building across the alley and found the gravel has been disturbed. It looks like the suspect got up to that building's roof and took a flying leap, landing near your terrace."

"He knew what he was doing," Liz commented. "You've installed motion detectors everywhere on this building except the roof. Which would have been useless since they can be set off by birds and debris that the wind kicks up."

"Yeah." Jackson scrubbed a hand over his jaw. "Did the guy have ID on him?"

"No," Liz answered. "He wasn't carrying a cell phone, either. And there's no vehicle parked in the vicinity that might be his. As soon as my partner and I get back to the cop shop, I'll run the guy's prints. At this point, he's a John Doe."

"Who wanted some paper so badly he murdered poor Silas Smith for it," Claire murmured. "He was ready to kill me, too."

Her expression solemn, Liz closed the cover on her

notepad and slid it into the pocket of her lightweight blazer. "Claire, you've had enough to deal with over the past couple of days, and I wish I didn't have more bad news. But I do."

Claire's eyes widened as she studied her friend's face. The aftershocks from her attack had kept her from noticing the strain in Liz's eyes. "Has something happened to Allie?"

"Not to Allie," Liz said quietly. "To Charles McDougal." For the second time that night, Liz gripped Claire's hand. "He's dead."

"No...." Shock struck Claire like a fist in the belly, making her hands tremble. "He...called me less than a week ago from California. Charles said... He said he felt fine."

"Ill health wasn't the cause of death," Liz said. "Ever since Silas Smith's murder, I've been trying to reach Charles on the cell number you gave me. When he didn't return my messages, I ran a nationwide 'check the welfare' on him and that monster RV he drives. Right before I got Agent Castle's call tonight, a New Mexico cop contacted me. They found Charles murdered and his RV ransacked."

"Murdered?" Claire shook her head. "How?"

"His throat was slit." Liz slid a tissue into Claire's trembling hands. "I'm sorry. I know Charles was like a grandfather to you."

The rush of grief Claire felt for the man who had taught her to love and treasure antiques with the same fervor as he, had tears burning her eyes.

"The cop I talked to said that Charles's computer is missing from the RV," Liz added. "He could have walked in on a burglar."

"Just like Silas Smith," Jackson said levelly.

Liz Scott met his gaze head-on. "I take it you believe in coincidence as much as I do?"

"If the answer to that is zero belief, we're in agreement."

When Jackson stood, Claire saw the tension in the way he held his shoulders, the hardness in his eyes. "Do the New Mexico cops have a time of death on Charles?" he asked.

"Early Saturday morning," Liz answered.

"Two days ago." Jackson shoved a hand through his shaggy dark hair. "I didn't recognize the guy who attacked Claire tonight. That doesn't mean he isn't one of Ryker's contacts."

"Ryker?" The tissue Liz had given her was now balled beneath Claire's fisted fingers. "Jackson, do you think he sent that man tonight? And had something to do with Charles's murder, too?"

"Anything's possible."

"How would Ryker even know about Charles?"

"Through me," Jackson said, his face as calm as carved stone. "When you and I were together, I not only talked to Ryker about you, but also Charles. I mentioned to Ryker how close the two of you were. How much I liked the old pirate."

Rising, Jackson laid a hand on Claire's shoulder. "I'm sorry. I know how much Charles meant to you."

Her heart aching, Claire blinked back tears. She felt as if she'd plunged into a nightmare that had no end.

"Liz, the only family Charles has left is his late wife's nephew. He lives in Maine. Do you know if he's been contacted?"

"The New Mexico cops finally tracked him down today. He's on vacation somewhere in South America. The nephew is making arrangements to have Charles's body flown to Maine for a funeral and burial next to his wife."

Claire nodded. "That's what Charles would want."

Jackson stepped around the couch, pausing near Liz. "If you don't get a hit on John Doe's fingerprints, I'll run them through an off-the-radar federal database I have access to. I'd also like to have his DNA profile when it's ready."

"Will do," Liz said and rose. "Claire, I wish I could stay with you tonight."

"You have work to do." When she shoved the comforter away and stood, Claire felt her legs tremble. She couldn't wrap her mind around the fact that Charles was dead.

"I can call Allie," Liz offered, her eyes crimped with concern. "See if she can get loose from that fund-raiser."

"No, she's planned that for months." Claire dragged in a shaky breath. "Just find out who killed Charles, okay?"

"I'll do my best," Liz said, then gathered her friend into a hug. "Call me if you need anything."

After locking the building's downstairs door behind the police and resetting the alarm, Jackson stepped through the open door of Claire's apartment and studied her.

She looked so alone, kneeling amid the books that had been tossed to the floor. And so vulnerable.

Just the thought of what the bastard could have done

to her tonight had Jackson's stomach knotted and his fists clenched. He could have lost her. Forever.

He sidestepped the clutter spread across the living-room floor and crouched beside her. "We can deal with all this mess in the morning," he said quietly, while breathing in the rich scent of Chanel that clung to her flesh.

"I want to do it tonight."

"Then we'll do it tonight." Because her voice was catching helplessly, he stroked a hand over her dark hair. "I'm sorry, Claire. About Charles. About everything."

"So am I." Gripping books in both hands she rose, turned to the bookcase and slid the leather-bound volumes onto an empty shelf.

Her breath was heaving, but she couldn't regulate it. There was pain, a terrible pain radiating out from her chest. She turned toward Jackson, his face blurred through her tears. "Why Charles? He was a sweet old man. He wouldn't have hurt anyone."

"I know."

"If he's dead because of me. Because of us. Ryker."

She pressed her fingertips against her lips and tried to will away her tears. But she couldn't. Any more than she could stop herself from stepping instinctively into Jackson's arms and burying her face against his chest. The tears she had tried so hard to choke back soaked into his shirt.

While she sobbed, Jackson held her close, whispering to her, brushing his lips against her forehead, her temple. For a few moments, he allowed the feelings free rein inside him—the need to protect her, to comfort her, the blind rage against Ryker and the feral need to avenge the deaths of his twin brother, the innocent old handyman and Charles McDougal.

To Jackson, it made no difference that he understood his ex-partner was fueled by his own savage need for revenge. Ryker had lost the two people he loved most, but to try to save his ailing daughter, Ryker had sold his soul to terrorist Hassan Kaddur who now had an unknown quantity of blank U.S. passports. Doing that made Ryker answerable for not only the deaths of his own wife and daughter, but possibly for uncountable Americans who fell victim to Kaddur's murderous plots.

Claire—and three men who were now dead—were innocent bystanders in all this.

He'd almost lost her tonight. Facing that reality left a hollow feeling in the deepest part of Jackson's soul. There was no escape from it, standing there with his arms around the woman he'd never been able to wipe from his thoughts—or his heart—and knowing she was no longer his. Would never again be his.

He'd never felt more alone.

When he sensed her calming, he murmured her name and moved his mouth from her temple to her tear-dampened cheek. Then she turned her head, lifted her chin and his lips met hers.

And when she moaned for him, it was like splashing hot whiskey over the coals of a banked fire. In the space of a heartbeat, his kiss turned frantic. Desperate. Driven by two years of missing her.

He lifted her hair to nuzzle the side of her throat, and felt her heart race against his.

Overwhelmed, Claire strained against him while she angled her head to give him better access to her flesh. A flood of longings, a storm of desires tangled inside her. Did she want this? Her body said one thing, her mind another. Her heart wavered in the balance.

The same heart that had been broken by the man holding her. The man she wanted desperately to lose herself in. The man who'd been unwilling to compromise so they could have the type of life together that would work for them both.

Memories shimmered, teased. The knowledge that the physical hunger, the *passion,* she once felt for Jackson was as strong as ever weakened her knees. And his arousal pressing against her belly was evidence his desire for her hadn't cooled.

Still, their wanting each other had never been their problem. They might want each other until the end of time, but that wasn't enough. Could never be enough, she reminded herself as she forced herself to pull away.

"Claire…." His hands still gripping the sides of her waist, he stared down at her, raw emotion glinting in his dark eyes.

"We can't," she managed over a suddenly dry throat and pressed a trembling hand to his cheek. "I can't be your lover again, Jackson."

"You're all I want." He dragged a hand through her thick black hair, fisted it there. His expression was set in almost savage lines, his eyes so bright they seemed to burn her. "All I've ever wanted."

"Don't." The ache in her heart was like a burning.

"We might want each other, but neither of us can be happy trying to live the type of life the other craves."

Jackson knew she was right—he couldn't imagine not doing the job he did. And since Garrett's death in the Barcelona bombing, his determination to hunt down Hassan Kaddur and other fanatics like him had taken on an even sharper edge. To do what he needed to do, he *had* to keep on the move.

He stared down into Claire's tear-stained face, his gaze settling on her ripe mouth. It would be best, he conceded, to remember how it had cut him to the bone when she had turned down his proposal and left him. Walked away. Only an idiot would chance going through that hell again.

"All right." He took a step back even while his blood burned for her. He swept his gaze around the apartment, taking in her possessions strewn across the floor. "What room do you want me to start on?"

"I…." Claire shoved her hands into the pockets of her coral slacks, pulled them out again. "The kitchen?"

"Fine."

Jackson headed that way, wishing he could clean up the mess that was his life just as easily.

Chapter 6

After his shower the following morning, Jackson followed the heady scent of fresh-brewed coffee to the kitchen.

Claire was there, standing with her back to him as she pulled utensils out of one drawer and slid them into another. She was dressed in slim white slacks and a turquoise blouse, her dark hair swept back and anchored with a tortoiseshell clip.

The only visible evidence of last night's attack was the small square of gauze taped to the side of her throat.

"Guess when I straightened up I didn't get everything back in its right place," Jackson said quietly.

Seeing her flinch at the sound of his voice had him setting his jaw. His years in the field had taught him that no security system was failsafe—there was no way to keep a determined intruder out, all anyone could do was make it noisy, time-consuming and difficult for him to get in. He would always blame himself for not checking Claire's apartment when they'd returned from the estate sale last night and thereby almost getting her killed.

"Sorry, I didn't mean to startle you," he said.

"I'm a little jumpy, is all." She slid both drawers closed, then turned to face him. Her eyes were bleak and her cheeks pale. Not just from last night's attack—he recognized grief when he saw it.

He knew his own sorrow over Charles McDougal's death wasn't anywhere near the tearing heartbreak that Claire must feel.

"Actually, you put most things back where they belong," she added.

"I've got a good memory." He swept his gaze around the kitchen with its butcher-block counter tops, old-time cooking implements hanging from overhead hooks and colorful rag rugs. "You haven't changed things much since I was last here."

"No."

Watching her open a cabinet and pull out two china coffee cups, Jackson's mind scrolled back to how she had looked on a sunny Sunday morning two years ago, standing at the stove, whipping up an omelet. One of his dress shirts, with a small ink stain on the pocket, covered her slender form. Her dark hair was a gorgeous, tousled mess from their lovemaking. She'd been barefoot, with bright-red polish on her toes. In silence, he'd stood watching her. And as he watched, he fell in love. All the way.

He had carried that Sunday-morning image of her with him for the past two years. Years he should have spent forgetting.

Claire pulled her bottom lip between her teeth as she poured steaming coffee into the cups. "Liz called while you were in the shower. She said they have an ID on the dead man's fingerprints."

"Did she give you the name?"

"No. She was still at her loft in the Montgomery, so she's coming across the square with the information. She said she'd stop at the bakery on the other side of Allie's shop and pick up muffins."

"All right." Jackson hesitated. "Are you planning on opening Home Treasures today?"

"Yes." She handed him a china cup nestled in a matching saucer. "I considered keeping it closed, but then I thought about Charles. He would want me to stay busy, to try not to think…." Tears welled in her eyes and she blinked them back. "Jackson, I can't believe he's gone."

Watching her, he sipped his coffee while need whipped through him. More than anything, he wanted to gather her into his arms. Soothe her. *Hold her.*

Last night he'd promised to keep his distance.

"Neither can I," he said quietly.

"I'm going to call his nephew to see if there's anything I can do." She flexed her fingers. "When the time's right, I'll arrange to have a memorial service so all of Charles's friends here can pay their respects."

Just then, the doorbell beside the shop's front door buzzed. "That'll be Liz," Claire said.

"I'll go down and let her in." Jackson set his cup aside, grateful for a reason to distance himself and give his system time to level.

Only when she heard Jackson unlock the apartment's front door did Claire allow herself to take a full breath.

A residual jumpiness from her assault and grief over Charles's murder had kept her awake all night. And underlying it all was her inability to wipe the memory of the kiss she and Jackson had shared out of her head. While she'd paced her bedroom, just knowing he'd been stretched out on her couch, ripe for the taking, had heat rising through her like mercury in a thermometer.

Greedy for comfort, desperate for his touch, it had been all she could do not to step into the living room and slide onto the couch with him. Because she knew while she was in his arms the years would dissolve, and it would be just the two of them, as it was meant to be.

But it wasn't meant to be, she corrected while she pulled an additional cup and saucer out of the cabinet. She and Jackson had tried living with each other and failed miserably. All the longing in the world couldn't change the fact they each craved a lifestyle that would never mesh with the other's.

"You've got one more for coffee," Allie Fielding said as she swept into the kitchen, her eyes filled with concern. In her habit of changing her appearance almost daily, the owner of Silk & Secrets had pulled her blond hair into a tight twist to enhance the Oriental look of her green silk Mandarin dress. Her salmon-pink toenails peeked out of strappy emerald sandals.

Allie plopped her leather tote bag on the whitewashed pine table in the center of the kitchen. "I was on my way here when I ran into Liz coming out of the bakery. She told me what happened to you last night. And about Charles's murder."

"I should have called you," Claire said. "It's just that—"

"You've had your hands full," Allie said, pulling her into a hug. "How are you?"

Claire eased out a trembling breath. "My nerves are a little unsettled."

"I'll bet. I'm so sorry about Charles. He was such a sweetheart and I know how much you loved him. How much he loved you."

Claire shook her head. "I still can't believe he's gone. That someone *murdered* him."

"It's awful. First Silas winds up dead, now Charles. And you get attacked. If I had been through what you have this week, I'd be a wreck."

"A total one," Liz amended from the doorway.

Allie gave Claire a final hug before releasing her. "I admit, I tend to get a little emotional during distressing situations."

Liz nodded. "If you'd gone through what Claire did last night, we'd have had to lace you into a straitjacket." Liz shifted her gaze to Claire, her pale-green eyes steady. "I'll tell you again, you did a good job of getting yourself out of that situation alive. Ike Bolton was one bad dude."

"Ike Bolton?" Claire asked. "That was his name?"

"Yes." Liz angled her head toward the door. "Castle took

my copy of Bolton's rap sheet across the hall to the storage room where he's got all his equipment. He's sending Bolton's fingerprint classification to the State Department to see if they've got something on him under an alias."

"And try to find a link to Frank Ryker," Claire added.

"Ryker?" Allie asked Claire. "Is he the rogue government agent who's out to get you?"

Claire held back a shudder. "Yes."

"But he's not going to succeed," Liz said, sliding a bakery box onto the counter. "Because Claire has pals like me. Then there's her own personal government agent who's watching her back. Like he did last night."

"A government agent who is a solid, muscled stretch of good-looking man," Allie remarked while pulling napkins out of a drawer. "So, just how bad a dude was this Bolton guy?"

"Really bad," Jackson answered as he stepped through the doorway and handed Liz some papers. "His rap sheet sounds like a pop quiz on the Oklahoma Penal Code. He's got arrests for robbery, forgery, narcotics violations, first-degree residential burglary."

"Meaning the owners were at home when he broke in," Liz explained. "Get this, Bolton was once hired by a security company that dropped the ball when it came to doing background checks on its new-hires. Bolton's job was installing alarms."

"Which explains how he knew to bypass the system here and get into the building." Jackson moved to the counter where Claire stood, pouring coffee into cups.

Instantly, her pulse began to pound, and she knew it

wasn't solely due to learning about Bolton's past. The T-shirt Jackson wore clung to him, revealing the breadth of his shoulders and the flatness of his stomach. His black hair was still damp, and with him so close she could smell his subtle woodsy cologne, with undertones of soap from his shower. Despite the current conversation, something passed between them, something hot and intimate, which had Claire tightening her grip on the coffeepot.

"Dead is a good thing for Bolton to be," Jackson added. His voice was calm, as if she were the only one affected by their closeness. Had she imagined the unspoken exchange between them?

"I'll second that," Liz agreed while she opened the bakery box. "Bolton's also got a juvie record that's sealed," she continued while handing out muffins the size of softballs. "Which tells me he's been on the wrong side of the law most of his life."

Claire passed around cups of steaming coffee. "Poor Silas Smith was the last person who could have presented a threat to Bolton, but he slit his throat anyway. I don't understand why."

"Not many people in the criminal world combine talents equally," Jackson explained. "As far as we know, up until a few days ago, Bolton was a thief, not a killer. Cutting someone's throat is messy and therefore not usually the method of a planned murder. More than likely, your handyman surprised Bolton, and cutting the old man's throat was done on the spur of the moment."

"That's my theory, too," Liz said. "So far, we haven't been able to determine that Bolton has any family. And he was never arrested with any associates, so there's no one we can squeeze for information on who might know what paper he was looking for here."

"Chances are Bolton's family information is in his juvie file," Jackson said while he sipped coffee. "You need a court order to get it unsealed."

Liz sent him a smug look while she broke open a muffin. "You feds don't have a lock on brains, Special Agent Castle. I've already got the ball rolling on that."

His mouth curved. "Good to hear, Detective Scott."

"Oh, I forgot!" Allie stepped to the table, crammed a manicured hand into her tote and pulled out a manila envelope. "Claire, since you closed your shop early yesterday to go to that estate sale, the delivery man dropped this off at Silk & Secrets. I'd already left to get ready for the fund-raiser, so my sales assistant put this on the counter with a note." Allie glanced at the envelope and her expression went bleak. "It's addressed to Charles."

With a lump in her throat, Claire accepted the envelope. "He was on the road in his RV all the time, so he had things mailed here." When her gaze settled on the return address, she sighed. "It's from the translator Charles always used. These must be more old legal documents."

"What kind of documents?" Jackson asked.

"From the 1800s and written in Spanish," Claire clarified. "Charles collected them. Well, sort of." She opened the envelope, pulled out several legal-size documents with elaborate scroll-work around the borders. "Do you remember Adam Navarro? He came into the shop the other day and bought some children's books."

Jackson popped a piece of muffin into his mouth. "The museum curator. You said he had some sort of feud with Charles."

Claire fanned through the documents and caught a whiff of musty, aged paper. Although her high-school Spanish was rusty, she recognized several property deeds and a marriage license. "They competed for these type of documents."

"Navarro and his wife were at the fund-raiser last night," Allie volunteered while nibbling on a bite of muffin. "Mitzy Navarro presented a huge donation to the foundation. As usual, all her husband did was strut around, showing off his inflated ego."

"I'm sure he'll be the same way Saturday night," Claire said.

"What's Saturday night?" Jackson asked.

"The art council's annual banquet. This year, Navarro's hosting it at the museum. I chair the banquet committee, so I have to go."

"Then *we'll* go," Jackson murmured.

Wordlessly, Claire laid the translated documents aside. Jackson was her former lover, her *ex-lover*. She had sweated blood while purging him from her life and she didn't want to be with him. Go places with him. Didn't want to continue feeling this yearning for him, so abrupt and acute it felt like pain.

When she looked up, she realized Allie and Liz were both studying her with an intensity that had warmth spreading through Claire's face. They knew each other so well, she was sure they sensed her unsettled emotions were more than just grief over Charles and the after-effects of the attack.

Out in the living room, the clock on the mantel tolled the first deep stroke of ten.

Allie checked her watch. "I've got to go. I have a bride-to-be coming in this morning who's commissioned me to design her entire trousseau."

"Sounds like you hit the motherlode there," Liz commented, finishing off her muffin.

Allie arched a perfectly plucked blond brow. "This, coming from someone whose wedding is mere months away, yet she's given zero thought to her own trousseau."

Liz shrugged. "Thinking about stuff like that gives me a migraine. Besides, why should I angst over pieces of silk and lace when I know you'll decide what I need and pick it all out?"

"Never fear," Allie said and rolled her eyes.

"Thanks for bringing the envelope by," Claire said.

"You're welcome." Allie shifted her gaze to Jackson. "Take good care of our girl, okay?"

"You have my word," he said over the ring of his cell phone. He answered the call while following Allie out the kitchen door.

When Claire looked back toward the counter, Liz had pulled the documents out of the manila envelope. "Claire, do you have the phone number of the guy who translated these?"

"No. Why?"

"Because Bolton wanted some sort of paper from you," Liz said, while shuffling through the stack.

"Do you think he was after one of these documents?"

"Anything's possible." Liz shrugged. "What did Charles do with his collection of these things?"

"He sorted them into categories and kept them in file boxes in his RV."

"Which was ransacked by whoever killed him." Liz pursed her mouth. "I'll check to see if the boxes were still there when the New Mexico cops impounded the RV."

"Liz, this doesn't make sense. Charles once told me the only value the documents have are for historical purposes. Certainly they have no monetary value. Why would Bolton break in here, kill Silas and attack me for something that's essentially worthless?"

"We don't know that he did. These documents are just something that need to be checked out."

Liz glanced over her shoulder toward the kitchen door. When she looked back at Claire, her expression had softened. "So, despite the murder and mayhem, how are things going between you and the yummy fed?"

"They're not." Claire flexed her fingers, unflexed them. "Nothing's changed from before."

Liz angled her chin. "From what you've told me about 'before,' you were head over heels in love with Castle."

"I was, and our relationship turned into a train wreck. I have no intention of climbing on for a second ride. I'm not sure I could survive that."

Liz rested a hip against the table. "A couple of minutes ago, you and Castle heated the air in this kitchen just by standing there, looking at each other. With all that boiling chemistry, you might not be able to stop yourself from taking another ride. If you do, just be sure to keep your seat belt fastened, okay?"

Claire opened her mouth to reply, then closed it. Hadn't she realized how little her feelings had changed last night when she stood in the warm shelter of Jackson's arms? It had been like suddenly having back a crucial part of herself she had spent years refusing to acknowledge was missing.

"Liz, I…."

The words died on Claire's lips when Jackson stepped into the kitchen, his face tense. "Claire, something's come up. You're going to have to keep your shop closed this morning."

"Why?" The grim tone in his voice had dread curling in her stomach. "Jackson, what's happened?"

"That was Tom Iversen on the phone. I need to go to his office at Homeland Security to view a tape, and I'm not leaving you here."

"A tape of what?"

"The first confirmed sighting they've gotten of Frank Ryker. He made it back into the U.S."

Several hours later, Jackson sat in a dimly lit room in Oklahoma City's Homeland Security office. Lining the walls of the small room were built-in counters that held dozens of monitors.

His attention was on the nearest monitor which played a grainy black-and-white surveillance tape. The tape had been recorded the previous day at a convenience store in a small town in northern Nebraska.

"That man on the tape doesn't look anything like the pictures you showed me of Frank Ryker," Claire said from the chair beside Jackson's. "Ryker has blond hair and a narrow face. This man is brunette and his cheeks are puffy."

When she leaned closer to the monitor, Claire's soft scent drifted over Jackson like a gentle stroke of hands, tightening his insides, just as it had done earlier in the kitchen while Liz and Allie looked on. He had realized then that the kind of primitive attraction he had always felt for Claire didn't allow for choice. They could each go their separate ways, agree never to see each other again, yet he would always want her. In his bed. In his life. Always.

"And he looks shorter than Ryker's six feet," she said, jerking Jackson's thoughts back.

"It's Ryker," he said, refocusing his gaze on the monitor to watch the man pull a soft drink can out of the convenience store's glass-door cooler. "He dyed his hair and combed it differently. His face looks fuller because he has cotton stuffed in his cheeks. He's got his shoulders hunched, which makes him seem shorter."

Claire sat back in her chair. "He sure fooled me."

"He would most people. But no matter how good someone is at disguise, they can't camouflage all their physical traits. The way they walk, hold their head. There's a thousand little mannerisms—no one can control them all."

"And no one would be able to spot them as well as a former partner," Claire added.

"Right."

"Ryker must know that police all over the world are looking for him. So I don't understand why he used his credit card to pay for gas and food."

"It wasn't *his* credit card. Not one in his real name, that is."

"Then how did Homeland Security get a hit on it?"

Jackson paused the tape, then shifted in his chair to face Claire. "Lots of federal government employees carry government credit cards—'G-cards' for short. Usually they're in the employee's real name. But certain employees like myself and Ryker who sometimes operate undercover have complete, working identities in false names, including G-cards. They look like a regular credit card any Tom, Dick or Harry would carry."

"If they're in your undercover name, where do the bills get sent?"

"To a mail drop or safe house. Then they're picked up and forwarded to the correct department and paid by the government." Jackson looked back at the tape. "Ryker has connections all over the world. Contacts who can supply him with new false IDs. I figure he intended to ditch all his government-issued IDs because he would know we'd be tracking all those names."

"*Intended* to ditch them all?" Claire asked.

"Usually Ryker is the coolest guy I know under pressure. But he's lost his wife and daughter. He's grieving, out for revenge. Emotions like that can't help but screw with his thinking. Keep him distracted."

Jackson hit the play button on the remote. "So, he gasses up at this convenience store and goes inside to grab a sandwich and a soda. Minutes later, in walks the Nebraska State Trooper you see on the right of the screen. Ryker's in disguise, he knows there's no chance the cop will recognize him. Still, the trooper's presence poses a threat." Jackson advanced the tape frame-by-frame. "See how Ryker fumbles in his wallet while he keeps the trooper in his line of sight? It's my guess that's why Ryker accidentally pulled out his old undercover G-card."

"Do you think he realizes he did that?"

"Good question." Jackson pursed his mouth. "If he didn't realize it right after he used the card, he would have by now. He'll know the State Department has flagged all his former IDs in the National Crime Information Center's database and his use of the G-card will light up the board."

"So, do you think that may make Ryker change his plans?" Claire said softly, her eyes huge and dark in the pallor of her face.

Jackson felt every protective instinct inside him rear up, tempting him to shield her by softening his answer. But he was the reason Claire was in danger. He owed her the truth.

"If you're asking if Ryker will change his mind about coming after you, the answer is no. He blames me for the deaths of his wife and daughter and he wants revenge against me by hurting you. If he has to wait one year, five years to circle back to you, he will."

"One year, five years," she repeated. "How's that going to work, Jackson?"

He knew she wasn't asking for an explanation of his ops plan. "You mean, how is it going to work for someone like me who can't seem to stay in one place for any length of time?"

"Yes, that's what I mean."

Leaning forward, he propped his elbows on his thighs. "I realize you think the concept of a home doesn't mean anything to me. But it does."

Because he wanted to reach for her hand, he linked his own fingers together and gazed down at the floor. "You know that my parents were geologists for an international company. That their jobs had them moving constantly around the world."

"Yes, I know."

"My parents had this thing about the North Star. It sort of started out as a joke, but it stuck because it was true."

"What thing?"

"Mom told Dad that he centered her, that she knew she could always depend on him if she needed him—he was her constant. And he jokingly asked, 'Your North Star?' So, forever after that when she looked up and saw the North Star, she felt centered. Home."

"And when you see the North Star, you always feel like you're at home?" Claire asked.

He started to reply with an automatic yes, then hesitated. Only lately had he begun to admit to himself how incomplete he felt. That whenever he gazed up at the North Star he no longer thought of home. Instead, his thoughts went to Claire.

Sitting beside her, while her soft scent drifted into his lungs, Jackson wondered if there was any possible way they could reach back over the gulf of two years and find what they once had. Or had the hurt each of them felt cut too deep to risk another try?

"Jackson?" she prodded when he remained silent.

"I feel something like that," he answered vaguely.

With his heartbeat thickening, he leaned back in his chair and focused on the monitor. On Ryker.

His former mentor. Friend.

Ryker was coming after Claire.

At this point, all Jackson could do was try to plot Ryker's route from Nebraska to Oklahoma City. A task that was problematic and haphazard.

"Claire, I want to teach you some self-defense moves."

She blinked. "I've taken a self-defense class." Her chin lifted. "And I managed to get your attention last night when Bolton had me. I think I did pretty darn good."

"You did great," Jackson agreed. "But compared to Ryker, facing Bolton was child's play. You need to learn different skills."

"What sort of skills?"

"I'm going to teach you to kill."

Chapter 7

On the drive back to Home Treasures, Claire was tempted to nix Jackson's plan to teach her deadly self-defense moves. Then her thoughts shot back to the previous night and she felt the ruthless press of Ike Bolton's calloused hand on her mouth. Her helpless struggle against his brute strength. The breathtaking pain when the tip of his knife gouged her flesh.

The warm trickle of her own blood seeping down her neck.

Reflexively, her hand went to the gauze pad taped to her throat. She'd been so debilitated by fear she'd had only a hazy memory of the moves she'd learned in the self-defense course she'd taken a year ago. It had been as if a sheet of ice slipped over her brain and she couldn't get through it. It was pure luck she'd been gripping her key ring and had had the presence of mind to fling it at the storage-room door to get Jackson's attention.

What if Ryker showed up and Jackson wasn't right there? Knowing how to defend herself lethally might be all that kept her alive.

That logic had her accepting the soundness of Jackson's reasoning. But she was surprised when he told her to meet him on her rooftop terrace for their first training session.

So, while the sun dipped toward the city's skyline, Claire slid her hands into the pockets of her shorts and watched Jackson shove her wrought-iron patio furniture to the edges of the outdoor area rug.

"I envisioned us training in a gym," she said. "With air conditioning and a thick padded mat on the floor."

He laid his holstered automatic and cell phone on the glass-topped dining table he'd moved to one side. "Do you think Ryker will wait until you're at the gym to confront you?"

"I hope he won't confront me at all."

Jackson glanced up while repositioning her chaise lounge with its padded floral cushions. "If I have any say in it, he won't."

Using one foot to move its wheeled stand, he rolled a potted hydrangea with deep-purple blooms the size of basketballs out of the way. He'd changed into soft-gray sweatpants that clung to his butt and thighs like a second skin. His black T-shirt with the arms razored out showed off the muscular contours of his chest and arms.

The sun blazing behind him added gold tones to his dark hair and bronzed skin. The thin scar that sliced through his left eyebrow enhanced his rugged image. As did those ice-blue eyes. He looked exactly as Allie had described him: a solid, muscled stretch of good-looking man.

Lord. Her pulse thumping, Claire diverted her gaze to the rooftops of the buildings on the opposite side of Reunion Square. It would be a lot easier on her libido if she didn't have personal knowledge that Jackson's physical stamina extended to lovemaking.

But she did know. And temptation had never been greater. Or as appealing. Or as arousing.

"You ready to take me on?" he asked.

She whipped around to find him watching her, those blue eyes locked on her like a laser. Heat skittered along her spine like an electrical current. With unsteady hands, she reached back to tug the band ponytailing her hair a little higher.

"Sure thing," she said and stepped toward him.

He gazed down at her, his expression as somber as the reason they were there. "Keep in mind if you're going to the trouble to fight, there's only one reason—to win. First, I want you to show me what moves you learned in self-defense class. After that I'll teach you strike points. If you hit them right, they're death blows."

"What if I don't hit them right?"

"You will, with practice."

She eyed him warily. "I'm just not sure I'm a candidate for hand-to-hand combat. I work out a couple of times a week at a gym with free weights, but I'm not exactly muscle-bound."

Reaching out, he played his hand along her upper right arm, testing for firmness. His mouth hitched up on one side. "You're somewhat toned, but you look like a cream puff. Which when it comes to street fighting isn't necessarily a bad thing. Any guy who grabs you will expect you to surrender quickly and maybe even start crying."

Her chin went up. "So, how about teaching me how to make *him* cry while I'm getting away?"

Jackson's mouth tightened. "If your opponent is Ryker, he won't let you get away. Which is why you need to learn to deliver fatal strikes at close range."

Claire swallowed hard while fear wafted up her spine like smoke. Since they now had proof that Frank Ryker had made it into the country, the possibility he might show up at any time was all too real.

He wanted revenge against Jackson, and she was the target.

"I'm ready."

For the next two hours they moved around the rug, adopting different positions and scenarios while she demonstrated each move she'd learned in self-defense class.

By necessity, their practice was close contact. Claire forced herself to ignore the sensations generated by having Jackson's hard-muscled body against hers. Refused to let herself think about the powerful control in his arms when they wrapped around her in various holds as he fine-tuned the steps she'd learned on how to break those holds. The scent of sweat and soap surrounding him enveloped her too.

By the time they finished reviewing and perfecting the moves she already knew, dusk was settling in, turning the summer sky a flaming orange. Heat hung in the still air.

"Now for the strike points," Jackson said while using the back of his hand to swipe at his damp brow.

Claire unscrewed the lid off one of the bottles of water she'd brought to the roof with her. She took several long swallows. Her gray tank top was soaked dark below her breasts and she could feel sweat against her back.

"How can we practice those moves if they're supposed to kill?" she asked while panting for breath.

"Relax, we won't be hitting each other," Jackson said before opening another bottle. "I'll show you some of the positions and striking motions, is all."

Helplessly, she watched his strong throat working as he chugged the water. Her nipples tingled an alert and a wave of heat that had nothing to do with the outdoor temperature swept over her.

In defense, she took a step back to increase the distance between them. She was about to take another one when he snagged her right wrist and tugged her to the center of the rug.

Facing her, he brought her hand up and caught her fingers, then held their tips against his neck at the small depression just below the Adam's apple.

"There's a single layer of skin over this area," he said. "It doesn't take a lot of pressure to jab through it. Then you flex your finger like you're pulling a trigger. That wraps it around the windpipe. When you jerk back, your opponent will be more interested in trying to breathe than holding on to you."

Claire felt herself go pale. "I'm...not sure I can do that to someone."

"Better your opponent dies than you."

She thought about her poor handyman and Charles. A lump of sorrow and regret formed in her chest. Maybe if they'd known Jackson's techniques, one or both might still be alive.

"Okay." She increased the pressure of her fingertip against the small depression beneath his Adam's apple. "Jab, flex then jerk back. Got it."

Next, he lifted her hand to the outside corner of his left eye. "Just a slight blow to this area of the temple can do major damage. Again, you use your fingertips, but you have to know the correct angle." He demonstrated on her, his fingertips pressing lightly at the corner of her eye. "You hit this spot right, you can cause memory loss, nausea, sometimes even death."

He showed her a few additional strike points on various areas of the body. Then said, "Now, practice what I just showed you."

He made her go through the motions over and over, using himself as her target. By the time the sky had grown dim, her arms ached and her hands felt stiff.

She flexed her fingers. "If we don't stop soon I won't be able to punch the keys on my cash register tomorrow."

Jackson glanced at his watch then flashed her a patient smile. "Okay, cream puff, let's go over the strikes one more time, then we'll get cleaned up and go grab some dinner."

"Cream puff, huh?" Lifting her brow in subtle challenge, Claire advanced on him, jabbing with more strength than she realized she had left.

The instant her finger connected with his temple Jackson spun away from her and bent at the waist, his hands propped on his thighs. His breath sounded ragged, labored.

"Jackson! Oh, God." She rushed to him, gripping his shoulders as if to keep him on his feet. Beneath her palms she felt him shudder. "Do you need a doctor?"

"No," he said through gritted teeth. He hauled in a breath, let it out. "Happens…all the time in training. It'll pass."

"I'm sorry." She as good as dragged him to the chaise lounge, forced him down beside her onto the padded cushion. Her palms settled against his chest, patting lightly. "I didn't mean to hurt you. I never meant to hurt you."

Jackson blinked hard. His system was still smarting, but it was her words that tightened his gut. She'd said the same thing that night in Cairo when she'd refused to marry him and told him goodbye. Her walking away had hurt a hell of a lot more than the blow she'd just landed against his temple with excruciating accuracy.

The press of her palms against his chest was delivering an entirely different kind of blow. Touching her for the past hours while they'd trained had been torture. More than once, his forearms had brushed her nipples. His hands had been on her legs, her hips. His body had slid against hers, and a couple of time while they grappled, one of his legs had been between hers. That was the kind of torture that made him want to get her naked and sink his teeth into her. And here she was, as good as sitting on his lap, her hands on him, her mouth inches from his.

"I'm sorry," she repeated, and he was suddenly cognizant that her breathing had gone noticeably shallow. And that her gaze had focused on his mouth.

He realized they were no longer adversaries squaring off; they were like the lovers they'd been two years ago. But last night he'd promised to keep his distance, so if either of them made a move, it was going to have to be her.

"There's nothing to be sorry about," he advised. "Any student who gets the best of her instructor should consider it a triumph. You've earned a reward."

Her gaze lifted slowly from his mouth. Despite the dim light, he could see the tiny specks of amber in her brown eyes.

"What sort of reward do I get?"

"What do you want?"

Claire knew she could probably come up with a logical, *safe* request if her fingers hadn't been splayed on Jackson's chest, making her aware of the sudden kick in his heartbeat. And the knowledge that only his thin T-shirt prevented her from raking her fingers through the tangle of crisp dark hair that she remembered vividly. Then there was the feel of his hard-muscled thigh against hers.

She didn't want this, the closeness, the temptation.

She wanted it more then she needed to breathe.

For an instant, the urge to retreat hammered at her. And then a storm of desire ripped through her and she tossed common sense aside.

"This," she murmured and, locking her fingers at the back of his neck, dragged his mouth down on hers.

His mouth was hot, and it was hard, and it was almost brutal as he crushed down to devour hers.

She reveled in the impatience, the heat, the hunger she felt in his kiss. She gave in to it, gave all to it, a moment's madness where body ruled mind and blood roared over reason.

With waves of pleasure engulfing her, she pressed against him. This was exactly what she needed. Hungry and fierce and mindless.

She felt his hands sliding over her, one moving up to shove into her ponytail while the other dipped low to grip one of her hips.

Clutched so tightly against him that no space separated them, she welcomed the intrusion of his tongue, wanted his mouth to stay on hers, fused with hers.

Wild, passionate thoughts spun in her head while Jackson's hand slid up from her hip. When his palm covered her breast, a thrill snapped through her like a whip, sharp, painful and with a quick, hard burn. Her nipple peaked against his touch while a groan sounded in his throat.

Claire's breathing quickened as if trying to outrace her heart. She knew nothing but spiraling heat and aching need.

She wanted more. She wanted everything he had.

When he pulled back, she gasped for air. She gazed up at him while the pulse in her neck throbbed and her body screamed for more.

"Jackson," she panted, clutching at him.

"I hear a siren," he said, his voice hoarse and ragged as he rose, hauling her up with him.

When they reached the edge of the roof and looked over, Claire realized that the noise she'd thought of as her body screaming for more, was actually the urgent whipping siren of the dazzlingly lit ambulance that had braked at the front of the shop next to hers.

"That's Allie's shop," she gasped.

"Let's go." Still gripping her hand, Jackson turned and headed across the roof.

He stopped only long enough to snag his holstered automatic and cell phone off the table.

By the time Jackson and Claire reached the sidewalk outside Silk & Secrets, the ambulance attendants had disappeared into Allie's brightly lit shop.

Only when Claire started to dash through the open door did she realize Jackson still had a grip on her hand.

"Hold on," he said, pulling her to one side of the shop's entrance.

Her throat tight, she tried to jerk from his hold. "Allie might be hurt," she blurted. Her mind swirled with images of Silas Smith, Charles McDougal, even Jackson's twin brother, Garrett. So many people dead.

"She might be," Jackson agreed tightly, holding his automatic pressed against his thigh. "If so, we need to find out what happened before we race in there." His face was tense, his eyes cheerless in the soft light from the carriage lamps that lit the sidewalk.

The sudden awareness that he was using his own body to block hers from view of the street stopped Claire cold. "Ryker? Do you think he's here? That he hurt Allie?"

Jackson's gaze remained on the shop's open door. "If he's here and he thought hurting one of your friends would get him access to you, he'd do it."

Just then, two muscle-bound EMTs wheeled a gurney holding a fiery-haired woman clad in a lacy red teddy and matching stiletto heels out onto the sidewalk. "Are you boys sure that I need stitches?" she asked while patting French-manicured nails against the gauze pad taped to her right temple.

"Yes, ma'am," one of the EMTs answered. The way his eyes bulged told Claire he was getting his fill of the woman's lush curves and endless legs.

Metal grated as the attendants lowered the legs of the gurney to the ground, then hefted it into the rear of the ambulance.

Allie bolted out of the shop, slamming the door behind her. She had a purse looped over each shoulder and a silk dress in eye-popping yellow draped over one forearm.

"Allie!" Claire eased around Jackson and gripped her friend by the arm. Even in the uncertain light from the carriage lamps, Claire could make out the red stain that covered the lap of Allie's green silk Mandarin dress. "What happened?"

"That's Mercedes," Allie said as the ambulance whipped away from the curb, its lights flashing. "She's one of my special evening clients. She insisted on having a glass of merlot while we started her fitting. And she just *had* to keep on those damn four-inch stilettos so she could see how they went with the red silk teddy."

Claire slid a look at Jackson. His automatic was now out of sight and his dark eyebrows were halfway up his forehead.

Allie shook her head, loosening blond tendrils from her topknot. "I stepped away from the fitting platform to get my tape measure. Mercedes chose that moment to start twisting and turning so she could get a view of her butt in the mirror. Before I knew it, she toppled off the platform and hit her head on the counter."

Claire gestured at Allie's dress. "The merlot splashed you?"

"And the Waterford wineglass shattered." Allie sighed. "I'm going to drive Mercedes's car to the hospital, then take her home. I'll cab it back here and clean up the mess."

"Give me your keys," Claire said. "I'll deal with the mess."

Relief spread over Allie's face. "Sweetie, I'll owe you big-time," she said dropping her key ring into Claire's open palm. "There's rug cleaner in the storage room that I hope will take the wine stains out of the carpet."

"Fingers crossed," Claire said to Allie's retreating form.

"What exactly is a 'special evening client?'"

With Jackson's deep voice coming from just inches behind her, Claire felt the now-familiar flicker of intense awareness crackling through her, tightening her belly.

And for the first time, she let herself think about what had happened between them on the roof.

What if the ambulance's arrival hadn't interrupted them? Would they have made love?

Yes. Because that's what she had wanted.

Oh, Lord, what was wrong with her? Why was she getting herself deeper and deeper into a situation that she knew had no future?

A sudden case of nerves had her hands sliding into the pockets of her shorts before she turned to face Jackson. "The Fieldings—Allie's folks—are one of the city's oldest and most prominent families. She grew up amid the cream of the social crop. That makes her an insider. The blue bloods trust her to be discreet."

Jackson lifted a shoulder. "In other words, she keeps their secrets."

"Right." He was standing close enough that Claire felt the heat of his skin. "Some men have both a wife and a mistress who shop at Silk & Secrets. It would be difficult if they both showed up in the shop at the same time."

"Yeah, catfights would be bad for business."

"Very. Allie doesn't judge her clients' conduct. She just tries to make things more comfortable for everyone involved."

"The mark of a good businessman. In this case, businesswoman."

"Exactly." Claire jiggled the keys in her palm. "I'd better see to that carpet. Then we can get cleaned up and have dinner."

When she turned toward the shop's door, he gripped

her elbow. His fingers were warm, tensed, and she felt a jolt all the way in her belly. "Does our getting cleaned up involve a joint shower or separate?"

She had a flash of memory from two years ago—Jackson and herself standing beneath a shower's pounding spray, him holding her while his mouth savaged hers, then his soap-slick hands moved down over her hips while he lowered her, guiding her legs around his waist as he pushed inside her.

In defense, she took a step back, freeing her elbow from his grip. It would be so easy—*too damn easy*—to wind up back under a hot, steamy spray with him again. To lose herself in the sensations of the wet heat of his body against hers, the dark hair plastered across his chest, the taste of him in her mouth.

The desire that she'd felt so strongly earlier hadn't lessened. If anything, it was sharper, more intense. She wanted to run from it.

"Separate showers, I think."

"You think?"

"I…yes." She glanced down the dimly lit sidewalk while gathering her thoughts. "What happened up on the roof is all on me. I basically attacked you. Twice."

"I didn't mind the second onslaught." Using the side of one finger, he lifted her chin, forcing her to remeet his gaze. His eyes were intense, unwavering. "If we hadn't been interrupted, we'd have made love. You know that."

"Yes, and it would have been wonderful. I also know that in the morning I would have regretted…everything."

His finger tensed against her jaw a second before he lowered his hand. "Why?"

"Because our being together would have been something akin to a one-night stand."

"The hell it would," he shot back. "Dammit, Claire, you know that's not true. What's between us means something. It always has. Always will."

In the wash from the carriage lights, she saw that his eyes were now hard blue ice.

She faced him squarely and shook her head. "What's between us isn't enough. A one-night stand has no future, and neither do we, Jackson. We proved that two years ago."

She moved to the side wall of her shop, patted the bricks. "*This* is my home. It's sturdy and lasting, with roots that are dug deep. I worked hard to have it and I'm not giving it up. *I can't give it up.*"

He stepped toward her. "Claire—"

"Let me finish."

He looked away, his jaw muscles flexing. "So, finish."

"All you have to do is tuck your head under your wing and go to sleep, feeling right at home, no matter where in the world you are. I tried to live like that, Jackson. I *wanted* to live like that so we could be together. But I couldn't. I can't." She closed her eyes. "I don't want to," she added softly.

Her last words punched an ache into Jackson's stomach that shot up toward his heart. His job had put him in numerous near-death situations, but this was the first time he'd felt shell-shocked. Granted, he'd known Claire had been engaged to the banker, but despite that, he'd never truly believed she would move on when he couldn't. Not totally.

Would it do any good to admit to her that his life had changed irrevocably two years ago when she left him? That since then obsessive thoughts of her had pursued him like hounds from hell? That nothing had ever been the same again?

Claire gestured toward the door of Allie's shop. "I'll get started on those merlot stains."

Was it pain he saw in her eyes? Or relief that she had admitted to him that she no longer had any interest in living in his world? "I'll be there in a minute."

Nodding, she disappeared through the shop's door.

Jackson closed his eyes. His lungs were burning and the sensation was rapidly moving toward his heart. He knew what he wanted. He had known two years before, but he hadn't gone after her when she walked out. How could he, when he'd known she truly didn't fit into his world? Known how unhappy living that life—*his life*— had made her. So he'd let her go.

But not until this very moment had he realized the full extent of all that he'd given up for his job. Thrown away. Lost.

His regret filled the air like invisible smoke. The only woman he had ever loved was totally and completely lost to him.

OFFICIAL OPINION POLL

ANSWER 3 QUESTIONS AND WE'LL SEND YOU
4 FREE BOOKS AND A FREE GIFT!

0074823 ‖‖‖‖‖‖ ‖‖‖‖‖ ‖‖‖‖‖   FREE GIFT CLAIM # 3953

YOUR OPINION COUNTS!

Please tick TRUE or FALSE below to express your opinion about the following statements:

Q1 Do you believe in "true love"?

"TRUE LOVE HAPPENS ONLY ONCE IN A LIFETIME."
- ○ TRUE
- ○ FALSE

Q2 Do you think marriage has any value in today's world?

"YOU CAN BE TOTALLY COMMITTED TO SOMEONE WITHOUT BEING MARRIED."
- ○ TRUE
- ○ FALSE

Q3 What kind of books do you enjoy?

"A GREAT NOVEL MUST HAVE A HAPPY ENDING."
- ○ TRUE
- ○ FALSE

YES, I have scratched the area below.

Please send me the 4 **FREE BOOKS** and **FREE GIFT** for which I qualify. I understand I am under no obligation to purchase any books, as explained on the back of this card.

I8GI

Mrs/Miss/Ms/Mr   Initials

BLOCK CAPITALS PLEASE

Surname

Address

Postcode

The Reader Service™ — Here's how it works:

Accepting the free books and gift places you under no obligation to buy anything. You may keep the books and gift and return the despatch note marked 'cancel'. If we do not hear from you, about a month later we'll send you 6 additional books and invoice you just £3.15*. That's the complete price – there is no extra charge for postage and packing. You may cancel at any time, but if you choose to continue, every month we'll send you 6 more books, which you may either purchase or return to us - the choice is yours.

*Terms and prices subject to change without notice.

THE READER SERVICE™
FREE BOOK OFFER
FREEPOST CN81
CROYDON
CR9 3WZ

NO STAMP
NECESSARY
IF POSTED IN
THE U.K. OR N.I.

Chapter 8

Detective Liz Scott strode through the door of Home Treasures five minutes after Claire opened for business the following morning.

Dressed in tapered black slacks, a black blazer and an aqua tanktop, Liz stopped at the front counter, her gaze sweeping the shop. "Where's the yummy fed?"

Standing at a round linen-covered table at the rear of the shop, Claire lit the last of the scented votive candles she kept constantly burning. "Jackson stepped into the back office to take a call from his boss."

Her throat tightened when she saw the serious look on Liz's face. Clenching the long butane lighter, Claire wove her way around tables and display cases toward her friend. "Has something happened?"

"I just received some results back from the lab." Liz laid a file folder on the counter near the promotional platter of assorted gourmet cookies the owner of Reunion Square's bakery had just dropped by. "It'll save time if I brief you and Castle together."

"Yeah, I understand," Jackson said into his cell phone as he stepped into view.

Clad in a khaki shirt and a pair of black chinos, he looked far more appetizing than any of the bakery's delicacies. Yet it was the shadows under his eyes that put a tug deep in Claire's belly. He'd gotten as little sleep as she had. She knew that, because she'd heard him roaming the living room while she tossed and turned in bed.

It had come as a shock to her last night when she'd admitted to Jackson she had no interest in attempting to fit into his world again. She hadn't planned to tell him that, hadn't *known* until that moment she had closed the door on them with such finality. But she had.

And now she felt the same throbbing sense of grief and loss and loneliness she'd experienced two years ago when she'd turned down his marriage proposal and left him in Cairo. It wasn't lost on her that she *should* be feeling those same emotions over ending her engagement to Brice Harrison, when in truth she felt a quiet sense of relief.

His expression tight, Jackson snapped his cell phone closed, then slid it into the pocket of his shirt. "There's been a second charge made to Ryker's government credit card."

Feeling her knees going shaky, Claire slid onto the long-legged stool behind the counter. "Is he getting closer to Oklahoma?"

"No. After he used the credit card in Nebraska, he headed west. The latest charge was for gas in a small town in Colorado."

"West." A crease formed between Liz's brows. "Is there a surveillance tape from the gas station?"

"No, it's a mom-and-pop operation with no security camera. Without a picture of who used the G-card, we can't be certain it was Ryker. He could have given it to a snitch or paid someone to use it in Colorado while he heads to Oklahoma."

"Is that what you think he's doing?" Liz asked.

"No. Ryker knows we're tracking his movements each time he uses that card. I think he really is heading west as a smoke screen."

Claire fisted her hands in her lap. "Why is that a smoke screen?"

"He has to figure that since I know his habits and the way his mind works, I'll be the primary agent assigned to track him. What he doesn't know is that my informant in Hong Kong overheard the phone call when Ryker mentioned your name. He doesn't want to tip anyone—especially me—to the fact that his goal is to come after you."

"He's leaving an obvious trail toward the west," Claire said. "A trail he believes you'll personally follow."

"Right." Jackson eased out a breath. "As long as Ryker wears a disguise and we don't know what type of vehicle he's traveling in, there's not much chance of him getting caught. All he has to do is obey the law, use out-of-the-way hotels, stay off major highways and not drive between midnight and six in the morning when the cops profile everything that moves."

Liz nodded her agreement. "Castle, from what you've told me about Ryker, the instant he switches his route toward Oklahoma, he'll drop off the radar. There won't be a trail of G-card charges to track."

"Exactly. If I were personally following Ryker's scent, I'd wind up somewhere on the west coast, scratching my head while wondering where the hell he'd disappeared to."

Jackson's expression tightened, a look with so much simmering beneath the surface that Claire suspected a lot more had gone on during the conversation with his boss than Jackson was letting on to. "So, Detective," he said to Liz, "I heard you say you got some results back from the lab."

"Right. Tests confirm that Ike Bolton told Claire the truth when he said he murdered Silas Smith." Liz flipped her heavy coppery braid from her shoulder to her back before snagging a cookie off the platter. "There are traces of the handyman's blood on the knife Bolton used to cut Claire."

Liz hesitated. "Tests also found particles of Charles's blood on the blade."

Claire felt herself go pale. "Bolton murdered Charles, too?"

"Looks that way," Liz answered. "Charles was killed in New Mexico a couple of days before Bolton showed up here and did Smith. Claire, you told me Charles kept the Spanish legal documents he collected in file boxes in his RV, right?"

"Yes, sorted into categories: marriage licenses, divorce decrees, property deeds. Things like that."

"According to the New Mexico cops who worked the scene, those boxes are missing. Presumably taken by whoever killed Charles."

"Meaning Bolton," Jackson said. "And since he had an interest in them, it's a good bet the paper he demanded Claire give him is also some sort of Spanish legal document. Most probably one in the batch that was delivered to Allie's shop instead of here."

"That's my theory," Liz agreed. "The first time Bolton came here, Silas Smith interrupted his search. Claire, then you, screwed up the second one."

"I don't understand why anyone would want one of those documents," Claire said. "Charles had some of them appraised, and they're basically worthless. They're mainly sought by genealogists tracing a family's history."

"One of them apparently has a different sort of value to someone," Jackson said. "It would help if we knew what specific paper Bolton was after."

Claire looked at Liz. "Did you contact the translator who mailed the latest batch of documents here?"

"Yes, and this is where things get even more interesting. He mailed all the documents Charles asked him to translate in the envelope you received the other day. The man added that he also assured Mr. McDougal that he'd mailed all the documents when he phoned him two days ago."

Claire blinked. "You said Charles had been dead several days when the New Mexico police found him."

"That's right. Charles was already dead when someone pretending to be him phoned the translator."

"Last night, I went over all the documents in the

envelope again," Jackson said. "As far as I can tell, there's nothing of any consequence in them." He met Claire's gaze. "Do you know where Charles bought this most recent set of documents?"

"I'm not sure. But the last time he called, he told me he'd purchased several items at an estate sale in southern California, and was having them shipped to me. The sale was run by a long-time friend of his named Leon Lovett."

Claire gestured toward the nearby mahogany table where a small wooden chest sprouting an arrangement of dried sunflowers and baby's breath shared space with pewter ale mugs. "That sea captain's chest was one item from the sale. Charles told me he has a potential buyer for it, so I'm using it here for display purposes. He also bought several leather-bound children's books."

"The ones the not-so-well-liked museum director, Adam Navarro, purchased?" Jackson asked, his brow creasing.

"Yes."

"Navarro said he has a sister who's opening a children's clothing and furniture store in Dallas," Jackson said. "Is that true?"

"Yes, Brice's mother…." Claire closed her eyes for an instant. "Virginia Harrison is a good friend of Navarro's sister. I've heard Virginia mention the children's store several times."

"Did you go through each of the books, page by page, to see if there was any loose paper stuck inside?"

"I always do that before I put books out for sale. There was nothing but a couple of small pieces of paper that had been used as bookmarks."

"Can you contact Lovett?" Liz asked. "Find out if Charles bought the documents at the sale he ran? If so, maybe Lovett has an inventory and we can find out if there are any documents missing."

"I have his phone number upstairs," Claire said. "If you two will mind the shop, I'll go call him now."

"If watching over your wares includes eating these babies, I'm all for it." Snagging a second cookie, Liz arched a brow. "You game, Agent Castle?"

"Sure," he said.

While faint wisps of vanilla from the burning candles scented the air, Jackson watched Claire walk toward the rear of the shop. She moved like a dancer in her trim white blouse and knee-baring slate-blue skirt that showcased her slim, muscular legs. Legs that had felt soft and silky against his while they had practiced self-defense moves. Thinking about the feel of her, and the way she had slammed the door on any hope of a future for them had kept him on edge and roaming the building all night.

And, early this morning, as dawn crept over Reunion Square, he had resolved that he would spend the remainder of his time here getting used to the idea that he had, literally and figuratively, to move on after Ryker was caught. There would be no reason to think he would ever see Claire again.

It was best for both of them, he told himself again for an uncountable time, then fisted his hands against his thighs. Dammit, if it was ideal, why the hell did he already feel empty and rotten?

"If your theory is right," Liz said, interrupting his

thoughts, "how long do you think it will be before Ryker drops out of sight and shifts his travels toward Oklahoma?"

Jackson forced his fingers to unclench. "Hard to tell. In fact, my boss isn't convinced that will happen. He thinks Ryker's got a contact on the west coast who can supply him with a new identity and a place to disappear to."

"Is your boss putting on the pressure for you to leave here now and go after Ryker?"

Jackson gave her a thin smile. "Sounds like you've got a direct line to my boss, Detective Scott."

"I just know how law-enforcement honchos think, meaning they try to figure out the quickest and cheapest way to catch do-wrongs. If your boss is like mine, he probably figures that sending you to the west coast to try to nab Ryker would be more time- and cost-efficient than your sitting around an antique shop in Oklahoma City."

Jackson had a sudden mental image of Ike Bolton holding the knife to Claire's throat. It could just as easily have been Ryker. "I won't leave Claire unprotected."

"Even if you do leave, she won't be without protection. She has me and the rest of the OCPD. But I admit, her having her own personal live-in bodyguard who sticks to her like cheese on a nacho is the safest thing for her right now."

Liz took another nibble of cookie, then angled her chin. "Your boss could always send you to the west coast and assign another State Department agent to protect Claire."

Liz's words struck him hard, because that scenario was more than a possibility—his boss had already hinted he might do just that. And every protective, primitive instinct

Jackson possessed told him to stay with Claire because Ryker would show up here eventually.

The sound of Claire's footsteps clicking down the stairs had Jackson turning his head toward the rear of the shop. The instant she stepped into view, his gut tightened with need and want.

If just looking at her had that effect on him, he knew that convincing himself to move on emotionally wouldn't be easy. But for the time being, he was going to have to shelve his feelings, keep his mind on the reason he had come here in the first place—to protect Claire from Ryker.

"Mr. Lovett wasn't home," she said as she moved behind the counter. "But I talked to his wife. She said one of his employees died, so he had to go out of town to the funeral."

"Died how?" Jackson and Liz asked in unison.

Claire held up a hand. "That was my first question, too. Mrs. Lovett said the employee had a heart attack while helping inventory items for a recent estate sale that Mr. Lovett's company oversaw. The sale was in southern California, so it could have been the one Charles mentioned to me. Mrs. Lovett will have her husband return my call as soon as she hears from him."

"Let me know what Lovett has to say." Liz glanced at the full-moon-sized clock on the wall over the cash register, then gathered up the file folder. "I've got lineup this morning so I've got to go. You'll be at the wedding tonight, right?"

Claire hesitated, then pressed a palm to her forehead. "I totally forgot about Karen Wallace getting married."

"You've had a kazillion other things on your mind," Liz said. "I'm sure Karen will understand if you don't make it."

"No, I want to be there. I'm supposed to serve cake and champagne with you and Allie."

With his attention partly focused on the front window, Jackson spotted two sleek brunettes approach the shop's door seconds before they stepped inside. Close up, he saw the similarities in the women's dark eyes and the shapes of their faces. Mother and daughter, he decided.

"Good morning, Mrs. DiCarlo." Claire stepped around the counter, greeting both customers with a warm smile. "It's good to see you again."

The older of the two gripped Claire's hand. "This is my daughter, Olivia, visiting here from Florida. I've been telling her about the Rapallo lace tablecloths you have in stock. She's dying to see them."

"And any Victorian doorstops you have," the younger woman added.

"I have a collection of doorstops, mostly from the Victorian period," Claire said as she gestured her customers toward a table in the center of the shop. "Several are cast-iron. I also have a few made of Nailsea glass."

Jackson breathed in the calming scent of vanilla while watching the women. For the first time, he understood that Home Treasures was the kind of place that made a person think of tradition and roots. Things he had never needed. Things he had never offered Claire.

"The wedding tonight is outdoors and casual," Liz said, pulling his attention back to her. "But if you don't feel like watching people you don't know get hitched, I can pick up Claire and bring her home." Liz's engagement ring sparkled beneath the lights as she gave a firm pat to the automatic holstered at her waist. "I'll be armed."

Jackson had no doubt that Liz Scott would put her life on the line to protect Claire. So there was no real reason for him to attend a stranger's wedding.

No *work-related* reason.

He glanced back at Claire, watched her rapt expression, saw the warmth in her smile as she handed a heavy piece of hunter-green glass to the younger woman. Claire belonged here, he knew that. And already he could see the remainder of his life spanning before him, and it didn't include her. Yet he would not, *could not,* let what had once been between them die out, not yet. So he would take all the time with her he could get now.

God, why couldn't everything be the way it used to be right after they'd first met?

He looked back at Liz. "I've never crashed a wedding before," he said levelly. "Might be fun."

That evening, Jackson steered his rental car through a manicured, upper-class neighborhood. "Since we're on the way to a wedding, how about giving me some background on who's getting married?"

Claire slid him a look from the passenger seat. It was just her luck he'd opted to pair his black slacks with a crisp linen shirt that matched his Viking-blue eyes. Eyes that were the same shade as the glittering water of the Mediterranean on a long-ago weekend they'd spent in the south of France.

Granted, she had glimpsed the water from their hotel-room balcony only during the few times they'd come up for air throughout those lust-driven days. Still, she remembered perfectly the water's glorious blue shimmer. And how crazy in love she'd been.

Been, she admonished herself. What she and Jackson had shared was over. She'd moved on.

Ignoring the ache in her throat where her pulse had begun to pound, she stared out at the tidy lawns and well-maintained houses that blipped by. "Karen Wallace is the bride. She's a widow with two grown children, and she works for Allie's foundation."

Jackson flicked a sideways look. "I thought Allie *sold* foundations."

Claire tipped down her sunglasses and peered at him. "Good one, Castle."

He flashed her a grin. "Thanks, Munroe."

"Allie not only owns Silk & Secrets and designs lingerie, she heads the foundation she established that helps victims of sexual abuse."

"That doesn't exactly fit the image of someone who sells sexy underwear to the same man's mistress and wife."

"Image is the last thing Allie's concerned about."

"How did she get into the foundation business? Sexual-abuse victims, not underwear," Jackson clarified.

"According to Allie, she grew up with potfuls of money and was the original party girl. Then in college her roommate was raped by a boyfriend. Allie took her to the hospital and had to testify during the trial. To lend moral support, Allie went with her girlfriend to counseling sessions. They were apparently a cold lesson in life's realities. Allie got serious about what she wanted to do with her life."

"Good for her," Jackson said. "So what exactly does the bride do for Allie's foundation?"

"Karen's responsible for the day-to-day operations. Her fiancé is a widowed doctor who does volunteer work in the foundation's clinic. His home is where we're going."

"Sounds like a happy ending for them both."

"It is," Claire said quietly as Jackson steered the car into the driveway of a two-story stone house with a wrap-around porch that sported pots of brightly colored flowers. Too bad fate wouldn't be delivering the same happy ending for herself and Jackson.

Several hours later, Jackson sat apart from the other wedding guests on a sturdy wooden bench, a tumbler of Scotch in his hand.

Miles of white netting, ribbons, paper wedding bells and bundles of flowers had transformed the doctor's backyard into the perfect setting for a wedding. Vows had been exchanged on the terrace. Toasts had been made and trays of canapés served. During it all, Jackson had kept well back of the crowd of people, using the time to observe. And think.

The middle-aged bride and groom had looked good together as they shared a long, full-bodied kiss that brought on cheers from the guests. They'd looked the way people were meant to when they were in love and facing a happy future. Soon after that, they departed for the airport amid a blizzard of rice.

Now, the sky was a dark-cobalt blue studded with diamonds. Moonlight poured down, mingling with the flickering lights of torches while celebrants milled around the yard with plates of cake and flutes of champagne.

Jackson kept his gaze on the white-skirted table where Claire and Allie served pieces of a three-tired wedding cake and Liz filled glasses from a fountain that bubbled with enough champagne to fill a pool. The close friendship between the three women was evident in the way they smiled and laughed together. Every so often, they would join ranks and dip their heads close as if divulging a secret.

He and Garrett had shared the same type of closeness, Jackson remembered with a stab of desolation for his dead twin. And, before things had gone to hell, he'd felt that same camaraderie with his partner. But Frank Ryker had sold his soul to terrorist Hassan Kaddur, and the nature of the job had never allowed Jackson to stay in one spot long enough for close ties to develop with anyone not on the job.

Or with a woman.

Until Claire. It had to be one of life's ironies that the one woman he wanted in the entire world couldn't deal with living places in scattered day-or-week-or-month segments, counting nowhere as home.

Through hooded eyes, he watched as she handed a plate of cake to a little girl wearing a lacy party dress. Claire laughed at something the child said, then planted a kiss on her nose and watched her scamper away with her cake. Seconds later, Claire pulled her chiming cell phone from the pocket of her shimmering turquoise dress.

Jackson felt a longing so deep, so intense, he had to set his jaw against it. Claire wanted children—when they'd been together, they had even talked about having their own. But Claire also wanted a yard for them to play in, with a picket fence and a husband who came home every night. Knowing that she'd spent part of her childhood living in a van with her mother, Jackson now understood her almost desperate need for roots.

And why she had turned her back on him and the job that sent him from one spot on the globe to another. She'd come home and found herself a steady, safe nine-to-five banker who could give her the roots and stability she needed.

So, why the hell had she called off her wedding?

He was still brooding over that when his own cell phone rang.

"Castle," he answered.

"Ryker used his G-card again."

Jackson narrowed his eyes at the sound of his boss's voice. "Where?"

"A small town in Utah. He gassed up at a convenience store. He's definitely headed west, toward the coast."

"Do we have tape from a security camera this time?"

"Negative. It was the same type of mom-and-pop operation as the store in Colorado."

"It's a smoke screen, boss. He'll head south toward Oklahoma any time."

"You can't be sure of that."

"I'm sure."

"We need every agent who has personal knowledge of

Ryker's habits out on his trail now. He was your mentor, your partner. You know him better than anyone."

"That's right. And I have no doubt he'll soon drop out of sight and head toward Oklahoma City. That's where his goal is."

"Claire Munroe."

"Exactly."

"Look, Jack, I'm not disputing that you might be right. But I've got a boss to answer to, too. And he thinks you need to be heading west, trying to pick up Ryker's scent."

"That isn't an option."

"It is, if that's what I assign you to do."

With tension coiling through his spine, Jackson shifted his gaze across the pristine lawn. In the flickering light of a torch, he saw that Claire had finished her own phone call and was now huddled behind the cake table with Allie and Liz.

A moment later Claire turned. Her gaze swept the dimly lit yard until she found him. And headed his way.

"Are you ordering me to leave Ms. Munroe unprotected and go after Ryker?" Jackson asked levelly.

"No. But if he makes one more charge to his G-card in a place that's west of where we know he was last, I will. If I do order you to go after Ryker, another agent will be assigned to protect Ms. Munroe. I'll get back to you."

"Right." Jackson snapped his phone shut and shoved it into his shirt pocket while he watched Claire approach.

Her dark hair was loose and mussed by the light breeze, just like it used to look when she rose out of bed after an interlude of nuclear-meltdown sex.

He swallowed, feeling pressure build in his throat. How the hell could he turn her security over to someone else, no matter how experienced the agent was, when just the thought of doing so tied his gut in knots? Dammit, this was Claire—it wasn't solely her safety he was thinking about. Where she was concerned, he felt protective, possessive and wildly territorial.

"You look lonesome here all by yourself," she said.

"I'm just watching the show," he said, gesturing for her to take a seat on the bench.

He saw the brief hesitation in her eyes before she settled beside him.

"Mr. Lovett just got home from attending his employee's funeral and returned my phone call. He's Charles's friend who oversees estate sales."

"Does he have an inventory of the items Charles bought at the most recent sale?"

"Yes, he read it to me. The small sea captain's chest, leather-bound children's books and a handful of Spanish legal documents were all Charles bought. Mr. Lovett's company shipped the chest and books to me, and Charles took the documents with him. Mr. Lovett will fax the inventory to me at the shop. It should be there when we get home."

"Then we'll know if all the documents Charles bought were in the envelope the translator mailed to you." Jackson pursed his mouth. "Did Lovett seem surprised by Charles's interest in the documents?"

"No. He told me Charles asked him years ago to give him a heads-up whenever he came across legal-looking documents written in Spanish from the 1800s. Over the years, Charles has bought any of those documents Mr. Lovett found. He said that at this most recent sale, the widow who hired his company to liquidate items her husband had collected had no objection to Mr. Lovett letting Charles in the night before the sale's official start to buy items at a fair price."

"The same way you did the other evening when you found that iron bed for Liz."

"Exactly. Letting pals in for a 'pre-sale' is nothing out of the ordinary in the estate-sale business."

"Did Lovett say if the widow had the documents examined by an expert before she put them on the market?"

"He doubts she did because she's filthy rich and doesn't need more money. Her main purpose for hiring Lovett to organize and run the estate sale was to get rid of her husband's collection of everything from toy trains to barbed wire."

"So, one or more of the legal documents Charles bought could have value. Whether he knew it or not."

"It's possible."

"One thing I'm sure about is that it isn't a coincidence Bolton took Charles's collection of documents from his RV after he murdered him. Or that Bolton held a knife to your throat while demanding 'the paper.'"

"If all the documents the translator mailed to me are listed on Mr. Lovett's inventory, maybe I should have an expert appraise them. That way we'd know for sure if one is valuable."

"Good idea." Jackson sipped his Scotch while his

cop's mind tried to connect the dots. "You told me Adam Navarro and Charles competed for those type of documents. And there was a professional rivalry between them that turned personal. Why?"

"Because of Charles's wife. She was a descendent and namesake of Rachel Donelson, Andrew Jackson's wife."

"*President* Andrew Jackson?"

"The one and only. Charles's Rachel had Donelson's personal diary in which she mentioned certain love letters written to her by the president. Rachel searched for years for those letters, with no success. Then, about a month after she was diagnosed with terminal cancer, the letters were found hidden in a false wall in a house in Virginia. When news of the find was released, Navarro used his formidable museum connections and his wife's money to buy the letters out from under Charles."

"Bet that didn't go over well."

"No, and Navarro refused to sell them to Charles, even knowing Rachel McDougal was dying and the letters would give her comfort. From that moment on, Charles hated Navarro like poison. When he found out Navarro had an interest in obtaining old legal documents written in Spanish, Charles put out word that he was a for-sure buyer whenever any of the same came up for sale."

"Did Charles know why Navarro wanted those type of documents?"

"No, and he didn't care. Snatching them out of Navarro's grasp gave Charles the sense he was righting the wrong done to his Rachel."

"The more I hear about Navarro, the slimier he sounds."

"I'm not looking forward to seeing him at the art council's banquet. If I didn't chair the committee, I wouldn't go."

The soft scent of Chanel pulsing off her flesh into his lungs was driving Jackson crazy. "If I see Navarro coming, I'll try to steer you in the opposite direction."

"I'll hold you to that."

They both grew silent, staring across the lawn. Having apparently served most of the cake and champagne, Allie and Liz had abandoned the table and now stood chatting with a small group of wedding attendees.

"The three of you seem more like sisters than friends," Jackson observed.

"We are."

"You didn't know Allie and Liz when I was around before. How did you meet?"

Claire glanced at him, a smile shadowing her mouth. "I'm not sure I should tell you."

"Why not?"

"Because it involves you."

He sipped his Scotch, watching her over the rim of the glass. "How so?"

"Champagne, a book of matches and your picture," Claire said, ticking the items off on her fingers.

Jackson stared at her. In the moonlight, her face was awash in silver light and shadow. "You got drunk and burned my picture?"

"We were more tipsy than drunk. And Liz lit the final match."

"Jesus." He scrubbed a hand over his face. "Sorry I asked."

Claire lifted her chin, stared up at the sky. "Jackson, tell me how to find the North Star."

"Why do you want to know?"

"Because from now on, anytime I sit on my rooftop terrace on a starry night, I won't be able to stop myself from thinking about it. And you."

Although she sounded less than thrilled, he felt a perverse streak of satisfaction. After all, she'd been interfering with his thoughts, both day and night, since she'd left him.

He set his glass on the grass, then settled his hands on her shoulders. "The first thing you need to do is face north," he said as he nudged her sideways on the bench. "Then find the Big Dipper."

"How do I do that?"

From behind her, he raised his left arm, pointed. "Look about one-third of the way from the horizon to the top of the sky. See it?"

"Yes."

"Now, sight along the two stars at the end of the bowl of the Big Dipper—they're called the pointers."

When he leaned minutely forward, his cheek brushed hers. Even as heat spread through him like a fever, he felt her tremble.

In the morning I would have regretted…everything.

Her words from last night hit him like a fist in the gut. He forced himself to relax, to strap back need. Dammit, he wasn't a glutton for punishment.

"A line drawn through them points toward the North Star," he said levelly. "Which, by the way, is the end of the handle of the Little Dipper."

"Okay. I see it now."

The huskiness that tinged her voice had his gut clenching at the same time she pushed up off the bench and took a step away.

She glanced across her shoulder, then looked back at him. In the moonlight, he saw nerves swimming in her dark eyes. "It…looks like the guests are starting to leave. I'll go grab my purse, and we can head home."

"Claire." He kept her in place with one quiet word.

"Yes?"

What would she say if he told her that, while watching the wedding, he had actually entertained thoughts of settling down? Of trying his best to give her what she wanted. Needed.

In a flash of memory, he saw the painful resolve that had filled her eyes the previous night, and he knew she wouldn't believe he could do it.

And, dammit, maybe she was right.

"Never mind." He stood, dumped the remainder of his Scotch on the grass. "It isn't important."

Chapter 9

Cell phone clamped against his ear, Jackson stood on the rooftop terrace while the sun dipped below the horizon. He'd last heard from his boss the day before yesterday while at the wedding. Since then, he felt as if he'd been standing on a fault line, waiting for the earthquake.

"Ryker's still moving west," his boss said. "I just got word he used his G-card this morning in northern Nevada. You're scheduled out of Oklahoma City on a military transport leaving tonight at nine o'clock your time. You'll land in Reno before dawn."

"I won't be on that flight." Until this moment, Jackson hadn't been sure he had it in him to lay his job on the line. Seems he did.

"That wasn't a request, Jack. It's a direct order."

"Understood." His stomach was clenched into a dozen tight fists. "If you send me to Nevada, you play into Ryker's hands. He wants every agent looking for him where he won't be. He intends to kill Claire Munroe. To do that, he has to come to Oklahoma City."

"You're guessing at Ryker's plans. You could be wrong."

"I could be right," Jackson grated. His shoulder and back muscles were like high-tension wire. "I *am* right."

"Either way, I've got another agent headed there. Miss Munroe won't be left unprotected."

"Ryker is coming after her because of me. *Me.* I know how he thinks. What he's capable of doing to her. I can't leave her."

"And I can't force you. Consider yourself on suspension, Jack. Effective immediately."

After a few additional terse words, his boss ended the call. Jackson snapped his phone shut and gritted his teeth on a curse. Stepping to the edge of the rooftop, he stared down at Reunion Square. With its swept sidewalks, wooden benches and flowerbeds brimming with pink and purple blooms, the square looked peaceful. Inviting. All that serenity would go to hell once Ryker showed up.

And, dammit, he *would* show up.

Feeling almost obliged to break something, Jackson whipped around and stalked toward the rooftop door. He had thought he could talk his boss into okaying his staying here. He sure hadn't planned on risking the job that defined everything he was. And with another agent coming in to take over Claire's protection, there was no logical reason for him to stay.

It must have been that damn wedding—it had done something to him. The Scotch probably hadn't helped. Then there'd been the warm scent of Claire's perfume filling his lungs while she sat beside him on that bench and gazed up at the North Star.

For the rest of his life he would look at the night sky and think of her.

Why the hell he felt as though she'd issued him an ultimatum to choose between her and his job was beyond him. Claire had done the opposite—told him quite plainly that, on a personal level, he'd already wasted as much of her time as she would let him waste. He wouldn't get another second.

By necessity they were sharing living quarters, but that was all. He was there solely because of Ryker—when that threat was over, Jackson intended to leave. He owed it to his brother to take down Hassan Kaddur, the terrorist whose followers had blown Garrett to bits in Barcelona, probably at Ryker's bidding. No way could he do that sitting at a desk in Oklahoma City.

And what in the name of heaven would he do if he *did* settle down in one spot? How long would it be before he had the itch to leave, more and more frequently?

Jaw clenched, he locked the door to the roof, then strode along the hallway to Claire's apartment. He started to reach for the doorknob when he saw a wedge of light shining from downstairs. He checked his watch; the shop had closed two hours ago so she must be working in her small office at its rear.

He strode to the top of the stairs, then paused. The

building was locked up tight, the alarm activated—he had no good reason to go down to her office. He didn't plan to tell her about the suspension. The threat of Ryker coming after her gave Claire enough to worry about. *Him* being up to his ass in alligators job-wise wouldn't help her nerves.

He raked a hand through his hair while his temper ebbed, leaving only frustration. In truth, it scraped at his pride to know she was no longer interested in trying to have a future with him. Everything was changing and he had to come up with a way to cope. Find some method to handle all this. Figure out how to stop feeling as if he'd lost some vital part of himself every time he left her side.

Turning his back on the staircase, Jackson stalked back toward the apartment.

Twenty-four hours later, Frank Ryker pulled an aging Chevy with hand-sized rust spots into a gravel parking lot dotted with equally derelict-looking vehicles. The bar in the dusty Texas panhandle town was a simple cube with shingle siding and dark windows high up, one holding an air conditioning unit that ground away in a monotonous drone. Beer signs provided most of the exterior lighting.

Inside, plywood booths stained brown to disguise the knotholes hugged the walls. Cigarette smoke turned the cool air hazy. That, along with murky lighting, made it impossible to describe anyone with accuracy.

Ryker shuffled past tables of wary-eyed customers nursing their beers to the booth at the bar's rear. Nearby was a short, drab hallway where a pay phone hung between the doors to the restrooms. At the far end of the hallway, an exit sign glowed a garish red.

With his hair dyed gray, shoulders stooped and movements that belonged to an arthritic old man, Ryker knew there was no chance anyone could ID him. Still, he'd made a habit of stationing himself with his back to the wall and near an escape route for too many years to stop.

Especially not now. He couldn't chance getting caught when he was this close to his goal.

Oklahoma City and Claire Munroe.

A waitress with bottle-blond hair that showed darker roots stopped by the booth. Over the racket of pool games and loud talk, Ryker ordered a beer, burger and fries, then settled back to wait.

And think.

He had never met Claire Munroe—all he knew about her was what Castle had said. And although she'd walked out on him two years ago, it had been crystal-clear he had never gotten over her.

He would never get over losing his wife and his teenage daughter. Leslie and Emily had been his life, his one true vulnerability.

Just thinking about them had aching loss surging through him. He barely acknowledged the waitress when she settled a long-neck bottle in front of him.

The first pull he took of ice-cold beer didn't do anything to loosen the tightness in his throat. Resting his elbows on the table, he pressed the heels of his palms against his eyes and pictured his daughter's youthful, innocent face.

One moment Emily had been the picture of health, the next a doctor was explaining how some insidious virus had damaged her heart and she needed a new one to stay alive. Her rare blood type made her chances nil at getting a transplant in the States.

Ryker gulped a swallow of beer. Then another. With no other option open to him he had used his connections spanning the globe and found a heart on the black market. He hadn't cared that the organ and medical expenses would top a million dollars—Emily's life had been worth it. He had committed treason by selling blank U.S. passports to Hassan Kaddur. Still, Ryker refused to think about the ramifications of his actions. He would have done *anything* to save his child.

If only Jackson Castle had died in the warehouse blast in Singapore. If only he hadn't remembered the one mention his partner made about the off-the-book safe house in Kuala Lumpur.

But Castle *had* remembered and sent a SWAT team there. Ryker's fingers tightened on the bottle. He would never forget the absolute helplessness that had gripped him when he discovered the Mobile Security Division had arrived ahead of him. Weeks later, his wife's and daughter's screams still jerked him awake on the rare times he fell into bouts of fitful sleep.

The lust for revenge shimmered through his fatigue, boiling through him like acid. It was the promise of vengeance that kept him on edge, fueled him toward his goal.

Claire Munroe. He would take from Castle what Castle had stolen from him.

In his peripheral vision, Ryker caught a figure moving his way. Keeping his gaze lowered, he watched a balding man dressed in grease-stained jeans and a blue work shirt weave toward the back hallway. He had a full mug of beer in one beefy hand and walked with the exaggerated care of a drunk.

Just as he came abreast of the booth he stumbled sideways.

"Goddammit!" The curse reached Ryker's ears at the same instant his table jolted and beer from the drunk's mug splashed one side of his face.

"Lookit wha you made me do, ol' man!" the drunk slurred.

Throttling back his temper, Ryker used a shoulder to wipe beer from his cheek and jaw. In one move he could have the jackass on the floor, but he couldn't risk making a scene.

"I'll be more careful next time," he said softly.

"Yeah?" The man's red-splotched drinker's face settled into a sneer that revealed yellowed, crooked teeth. "Why wait till next time?" he asked and reared his fisted hand back.

Swinging a leg out, Ryker kicked the man on the inside of his knee. His leg went out from under him and he lurched forward. Ryker hit him on the bridge of the nose. Cartilage crunched; the drunk went down, his forehead ramming against the edge of the table before he hit the floor like a sack of sand.

A quick cessation of conversation told Ryker that every person within range of vision was looking his way.

His gaze whipped behind the bar to where the tattooed bartender already had the phone to his ear.

Although he carried forged ID with photos that matched his present appearance, Ryker had no desire to chat with a cop. If luck was with him, the police wouldn't bother hunting down someone who'd been assaulted in a bar that was a watering hole for derelict blue-collar workers.

Sliding out of the booth, Ryker dug a bill out of his pants pocket and tossed it on the tabletop. Then he turned and headed for the rear door.

At the same time Frank Ryker drove away from the nondescript bar in the Texas panhandle, Claire checked her appearance in her bedroom's full-length mirror.

She'd drawn her hair back on one side with a rhinestone-studded comb; her black cocktail dress with wire-thin straps accentuated her figure. The makeup she had taken painstaking care to apply hid the shadows under her eyes that came from too many restless nights.

Overall, she looked calm and serene, she decided. No one looking at her would suspect that a rogue government agent wanted to kill her. Or that another government agent was slowly driving her crazy.

Staring at her reflection, a dry ache settled in Claire's throat. Since the night of the wedding, she had sensed a decided change in Jackson. It was as if some unnamed emotion had begun brewing inside him. The distance he'd put between them wasn't the physical kind—that would have been impossible to do while he slept on her couch and escorted her to weddings and tonight's art council benefit. Still, the wall was there.

And the more impenetrable it became, the more urgency she felt to knock it down.

Which was ridiculous, she told herself as she grabbed her black beaded purse off her bed. She *wanted* the distance. Had insisted on it.

Squaring her shoulders, she pulled open the bedroom door and stepped into the hallway. When she glanced into the living room, everything inside her went still.

Jackson stood in front of the fireplace, his gaze focused out a window while he talked on his cell phone. The sight of his tall, lean form clad in a black tuxedo had the impact of a jolt of electricity. It was beyond her how a man could look as much at home in a black tux as he did in worn denim and khaki. And if the tux wasn't unsettling enough, he had yet to get around to getting a haircut. His tanned face and intense blue eyes, combined with the raven-black hair that curled over the collar of his white formal shirt gave him a rakish look.

Devastating.

And dangerous.

Hoping for a measure of calm, she pulled in a deep breath, which only filled her lungs with the woodsy fragrance of his aftershave. Why, she wondered, couldn't she cut the last of the strings that bound Jackson Castle to her heart?

Although she'd made no sound, he must have sensed her presence because he swung around abruptly. With the phone still pressed against one ear, his gaze focused on her. Those piercing blue eyes traveled down, all the way to her black, strappy heels then back up again.

His intense examination settled heat at the base of her spine while anxiety built in her belly. She didn't want to be haunted by old, impossible longings for a man whose life would never meld with hers.

When the heat in her blood intensified, she realized that what she wanted didn't matter. The need refused to be shoved aside.

So simple. So cut-and-dried.

So impossible.

Struggling to get a grip on her composure, she adjusted the purse's chain over her shoulder while Jackson ended his phone call.

His grim expression had her frowning as she moved to one end of the couch. "Was that your boss? More news about Ryker?"

"No to both questions. It was Tom Iverson at Homeland Security. There's nothing new on Ryker. His last use of the G-card was two days ago in northern Nevada."

"He could be anywhere by now." A chill went down Claire's spine like an icy finger. "Here."

"It's possible." Jackson's tone was all business, his mouth set in a firm line. "Look, I know you can't help but worry about Ryker. But you're chairman of the committee overseeing the art benefit, so you'll have plenty to deal with once we get to the museum. How about letting me do the worrying, at least for tonight?"

"I'll try." She forced a smile. "I guess the silver lining

is that you'll have something to keep your mind occupied. Otherwise, all the talk about art and fund-raising would probably have you bored to death."

"I've got one other thing on my agenda for tonight."

"What?"

"A chat with Adam Navarro. He collects old legal documents written in Spanish. Ike Bolton might not have said that was the paper he was after while he held a knife to your throat, but my gut tells me it was."

"Do you think Navarro's somehow connected with Ike Bolton?" Claire felt a shudder ripple through her. It was hard just saying the name of the man who had attacked her, killed her handyman and murdered Charles.

"Liz hasn't had any luck finding a link between Navarro and Bolton," Jackson answered. "Her questioning Navarro now might put him on the defensive, which is where Liz doesn't want him in case a connection surfaces later. She knew I'd see him tonight at the museum, so she asked me to mention Charles. See what sort of reaction I get."

"You don't think that will make Navarro suspicious?"

"The day I met him in the shop, I told him I was a geologist. Navarro won't have any reason to think I'm doing anything more but making conversation."

Claire nodded just as the clock on the mantel began to strike in deep, heavy bongs.

"Ready to go?" Jackson had swung open the apartment door and stood waiting for her.

That was the picture of him she had to keep in the forefront of her mind, she reminded herself. Jackson Castle,

standing at an open door, always on the way to somewhere else.

Later that evening, Jackson stood in an exhibit hall of
the National Cowboy and Western Heritage Museum
while tuxedo-clad men and elegantly gowned women
milled around the art-lined hall. The majority of guests
sipped wine while gazing at bronze sculptures by an artist
purported to be the next Frederic Remington.

Off to one side of a display of priceless old-West
firearms, Claire spoke in low tones to a slim blonde with
a PDA tucked discreetly into the palm of one hand. So
far, Claire's duties as chairman of the art council's fund-
raising committee had kept her and her assistant occupied
since the moment they arrived.

The entire time, Jackson had kept Claire in his sights.
Which gave him plenty of time to imagine himself
sliding the straps of that slim, black dress off her shoulders. And shoving his hands through her dark, glossy
hair to free it from the comb that glittered like stars
beneath the bright lights.

Although he'd made a concerted effort not to picture
what she looked like beneath the dress, he had failed
miserably. How the hell was he supposed to forget *her*
while plagued with memories of the soft texture of her
skin, the taste of her mouth, the small sounds that purred
in her throat when she reached for him, opened for him?

He took a long swallow of the tonic water he'd picked
up at one of the bars dotting the various exhibit halls.
Twenty-four hours had passed since his boss had sus-

pended him, and the passage of time had stoked his anger like a blast furnace. Dammit, he *knew* he was right about Frank Ryker. The rogue agent was coming after Claire, but there was no way to prove it until the bastard made an appearance. Meanwhile, Jackson had no choice but to keep Claire close. Physically near. And sleep on her damn couch when all he wanted was to slide into her bed and bury himself in her warm depths.

The blonde finished stabbing buttons on her PDA, then turned and melted into the crowd. Claire smiled at two gray-haired men checking out the firearms display, then began working her way through the sea of bodies, stopping occasionally to speak to various guests.

With raw frustration brewing inside him, Jackson shifted his gaze just as Adam Navarro stepped through the exhibit hall's arched entry. With his dark hair glinting beneath the generous spill of light, the curator looked very large and very solid in his expensively cut tuxedo.

"Jackson Castle, Mr. Navarro," Jackson said over the hum of conversation and laughter. "We met the other day at Home Treasures."

Navarro gripped the hand Jackson offered. "You've got a good memory, Mr. Castle."

"It comes in handy from time-to-time."

"When we met at Claire's shop, I didn't realize you would be attending this benefit with her." Navarro's smile was as smooth as his voice.

"My business in Oklahoma City is taking longer than I expected. I was at loose ends tonight, so Claire invited me to come along."

"I haven't had a chance to speak to her yet tonight." Navarro looked suddenly thoughtful. "I understand that Brice Harrison canceled the reservation for the hall here that he and Claire planned to use for their wedding reception. I don't mean to pry, Mr. Castle, but does your presence have anything to do with the wedding being called off?"

"Claire and I are old friends, that's all."

"Then it's fortunate your business is keeping you here longer, as I'm sure Claire needs support just now. Canceling her wedding would be difficult enough to deal with. Add to that two recent deaths of people she knows, and I imagine she's having a hard time coping."

Jackson sipped his tonic water. So much for his having to figure out a casual way to bring up Charles McDougal's murder so as not to arouse Navarro's suspicions.

"Finding a handyman with his throat cut in his or her shop would be a shock to any business owner," Jackson agreed. "Learning that McDougal had been murdered hit Claire with a double whammy."

"I can imagine, since they were so close." Navarro pursed his mouth. "Do the police know why he was murdered?"

"Right now the theory is he walked in on a burglary in progress. His RV was ransacked and there was property missing."

"Property?"

Interesting, Jackson thought, that Navarro was pumping *him.* "McDougal's computer was taken. And boxes of Spanish legal documents."

Navarro's dark eyebrows registered brief surprise. "Taking the computer is understandable, since it can be sold or pawned. But the murderer taking those documents doesn't make a lot of sense."

"Why not?"

"Charles McDougal and I shared an interest in collecting old legal documents written in Spanish. They have little or no value."

"Then why collect them?"

"I'm compiling my family's genealogy. The Navarros have a rich history in Mexico and Texas, so once in a while I find a legal document about a wedding or land acquisition that helps me add information to an ancestor's background. Old letters, newspapers and legal documents are often the only way to connect the dots when you're trying to collect history on a long-dead relative."

"Makes sense," Jackson said. "McDougal is far from a Latin-American name. Why did Charles collect the same kind of documents if they're essentially worthless?"

"I don't believe he ever said. Perhaps Claire can answer that question for you."

As he spoke, Navarro's gaze went past Jackson's shoulder and registered another flash of quick surprise. "There she is now. Do you know the man she's talking to?"

Jackson's gaze followed the curator's. Claire stood with her back to him, so he couldn't gauge her expression. But he saw clearly the tall sandy-haired man whose face looked lean and faintly aristocratic, with well-defined bones and a long, straight nose. He stood inches from Claire, his hand wrapped around hers while he gazed down at her with desire and yearning. Seconds later, his head dipped, her chin lifted. Their lips brushed.

A surge of dangerous emotion whipped through Jackson. He'd seen the man once before, when he'd left Claire's apartment on the night she'd broken their engagement.

Trying to ignore the kink in his gut, Jackson looked back at Navarro. "Yeah, I know who the guy is."

"From the look on Brice's face, their body language, I'd guess that whatever they're discussing is personal. And very serious," Navarro speculated with a smile. "Perhaps the wedding will take place after all?"

Ancient instincts surged to the fore, making Jackson want to plow through the well-groomed guests, pull Claire into his arms and stake a claim that no other man could dismiss. Instead, he held himself back. She no longer belonged to him, had made it clear that she didn't want history to repeat itself.

"You could be right." He tossed back the last of his tonic water and wished it were Scotch. "Looks like there might be a wedding after all."

Chapter 10

By the time Jackson parked his rental car behind Home Treasures, his jaw was locked tight enough to cramp. Replaying in his brain was the image of Claire standing amid a sea of formally clad art patrons while she gazed up at her ex-fiancé. And the look of abject love on banker boy's face when he'd dipped his head and brushed his mouth against hers.

When she'd finally extricated herself from Brice Harrison and showed back up at *his* side, Jackson had noted the rush of color staining her throat and cheeks. And he sure as hell hadn't missed the way she tensed against his touch each time he pressed his palm at the small of her back while they moved through the museum's various exhibition galleries.

She'd had very little to say to him during the remainder of the art council benefit. And on the drive home from the museum, the atmosphere in the car had been as relaxed as a coiled snake.

"Everything all right?" he asked after he escorted her inside her building's back door and reset the alarm.

"Peachy." Without meeting his gaze, she headed up the staircase. Beneath her black cocktail dress, her spine was as stiff as a knife blade, her shoulders squared.

By the time they reached the door to her apartment, the tension inside Jackson was like a live wire, sparking with dangerous electricity.

In silence, he watched her dig her key out of her beaded bag, twist it in the lock. When she started to push open the door, he gripped her elbow.

"I need to check out the apartment before you go in."

Her fingers grazed the small bandage covering the spot where Bolton's knife dug into her flesh. "I'll wait here."

Jackson narrowed his eyes. He thought he'd heard the edge of tears in her voice, but he wasn't sure. And gut instinct told him this wasn't the time to ask.

After performing a quick reconnoiter of the apartment he returned to the front door. "All clear."

Claire swept passed him. She got halfway across the living room, then ground to a stop and turned. Her face was pale, her dark eyes glistening, confirming she was struggling not to cry.

Another vision of the banker kissing her tape-looped in Jackson's head. The fact she was close to tears over another man had a greasy pool of jealousy churning in his gut. When she'd left him two years ago, he had known she would eventually find someone else. But during that time, he'd purposely immersed himself in his work, requested assignments on other continents. That had saved him from having to watch the woman that every inch of his being still considered *his* with another man.

Seeing that very thing up close and personal tonight scraped at his insides like tiny claws.

Claire wrapped her arms around her waist. "You'd think with every cop in the country looking for Ryker, someone would have caught him by now."

Jackson flexed his fingers, unflexed them. "It can't be soon enough."

"Because you want to leave," she said, the rawness of her emotions unraveling in her voice. "The minute he's caught, you'll leave."

Suspecting the comment was as loaded as the automatic holstered at the small of his back, Jackson remained silent for a moment. "Isn't that what you want?" he asked finally.

"That's a strange question coming from a man who has never let what I want matter."

"Claire—"

Without waiting for him to finish, she whipped around and headed down the dark hallway. Seconds later, her bedroom door slammed shut with enough force to make the pictures on the walls shimmy.

Holding himself back from going after her, Jackson struggled for calm while he dragged off his tuxedo jacket, tossed it across the back of the couch. He jerked his bow tie loose, telling himself that it'd be smart to figure out what he'd done to set her off before he made a move.

Smart lasted until he heard the sharp snap as she engaged the lock on her bedroom door. It was the first time since he'd arrived that she'd found it necessary to lock him out.

What the hell did she think he was going to do? Force himself on her? Strip that sexy black dress off her lush body and plunge into the cradle of her wet flesh, which in truth was what he'd been aching to do the entire damn evening?

More like the entire time he'd been back in Oklahoma City.

Too pent-up now to keep still, he followed the path she'd taken across the living room and down the hallway. Even though he knew her bedroom door was locked, he gripped the doorknob and jiggled it.

"You want to tell me exactly what I did to piss you off?"

"Everything!" Claire tossed the word across her shoulder. With moonlight pouring in through the lace curtains, she hadn't bothered turning on the light before she'd started pacing the length of her small, cozy bedroom.

Of course she had known she would run into Brice tonight—he sat on the museum's board of directors, so his presence there had been inevitable. But she hadn't known until an instant before his lips brushed hers that he intended to kiss her. Hadn't known that that one feather-light contact would zoom the swirling emotions that had plagued her for days into sharp, clear focus.

While she stood there staring up at Brice, it was as if her mind suddenly heard what her heart had been trying to tell her: she could never be happy with Brice—or any other man—because she was in love with Jackson Castle. Had never stopped loving him.

"Let's attempt to narrow this down." Jackson's gruff voice boomed through the door while Claire blinked furiously, trying to discourage the tears that had threatened to fall since that realization rose inside her like a tidal wave, demanding to be let out.

She dug her nails into her palms and continued pacing. Dammit, she didn't want to love Jackson. Had tried so hard not to. Had actually thought she was over him. Most likely would have managed to kid herself into believing that for the rest of her life if he hadn't come back. But he had, and he was standing just on the other side of her bedroom door. And, holy heaven, she wanted him.

He was all she wanted.

"Things were fine between us until you hooked up with Harrison at the museum," Jackson continued. "Locked lips with the guy in front of God and everybody."

"That's *my* business."

"Not when it has you barricading your bedroom door against me. Dammit, Claire, if Harrison's who you want, why don't you marry him and put him out of his misery?"

"Because he's not you!" she blurted while advancing toward the door.

Instantly, she pressed her fingertips against her lips. She hadn't meant to tell him that, but there were no lies in her tonight. Not when the truth was right there, staring her in the face.

"I thought you…didn't want me. Us." Jackson's voice was now a husky murmur through the wood. "After you gave me my walking papers, I thought you moved on."

Her fingers gripped the doorknob. "I thought so, too."

With misery rolling through her, Claire leaned her forehead against the door. It was crazy, but standing there in the dark, she could swear she could smell the intensely masculine scent of Jackson's aftershave through the wood. There was no escaping the heat that swept through her, or the empty feeling of aloneness.

"I will move on…eventually," she said, her voice a dusty little whisper. At least she hoped so.

"What did you say?"

She dragged in a deep breath. "I said you should go. Have your boss send another agent to protect me in case Ryker does come here. It would be best for both of us if you leave here, Jackson."

"My boss suspended me."

"What?" Claire eased her head back and stared at the door as if she could glimpse his expression through it. "Why?"

"He ordered me to leave here and go after Ryker. I said no."

"Because I would have been left unprotected?"

"No. He was going to send another agent here in my place."

"Then why didn't you go?"

"Ryker is after you because of me. I won't leave you, Claire."

For the space of a heartbeat she went utterly still,

breath jammed in her throat. Then she undid the lock and wrenched open the door.

One forearm braced on the jamb, Jackson stood in silence, making no move to touch her. He'd taken off his jacket and the tails of his black bow tie hung down the front of his crisply pleated shirt. He watched her steadily, his eyes so dark, they didn't look blue at all.

"I can't leave you," he said softly. "Not while you're in danger."

Her fingers tightened on the edge of the door. "Did you know you'd be suspended if you refused your boss's orders?"

"I knew it was a possibility."

"And after Ryker's caught, what happens with your job?"

"I don't know. My boss left things up in the air."

"So, he might let you go back to work?"

"Yes." Jackson pushed away from the doorjamb and stepped forward. "If I do go back, that doesn't mean I'll be moving on from you. After you left me, I never even tried. Ryker knows that. He blames me for the deaths of two people he loves, so he targeted the two people I care about the most in the world. My twin brother and you."

Jackson reached out and caught a stray lock of her hair, letting it drift through his fingers. "When I asked you to marry me, I wanted you for a lifetime. Forever. That hasn't changed."

Claire's pulse thrummed when she saw the truth of his words in his eyes. She was so weary, so emotionally battered that tonight the truth was all that mattered.

She pressed an unsteady hand over the center of his

chest and felt his heart beat against her palm. "I'm tired of telling myself I don't feel something that I do. I thought I was over you. God knows I wanted to be. I found out tonight I'm not."

"Sounds like we both have the same problem," he said as his hands framed her face.

"Sounds like." Her senses were roiling and his touch had set her body on fire. Right now, she no longer cared that he might leave again. Didn't give a flip that if he did, he would walk away with more of her heart. All she cared about was now, this man.

Her hands rose, braceleted his wrists. "How about we don't talk about what doesn't work between us?"

"Good idea," he said quietly. "What do you want to talk about?"

"What does work. What always did." She pressed her body against his and responded to him as if she were dying of thirst and he were the well. "Take me to bed, Jackson."

"You're sure?" His voice was so husky her own throat tightened in reaction.

"Yes."

His thumbs brushed against her throat and she felt herself tremble. "Knowing that I might leave again, go back to the same job, you're sure this is what you want?"

"I'm sure I need you," she said, the pulse-point in her throat beating against his thumbs. "That I want you. I've never been more sure."

Hard and aching, Jackson curved his hands over her bottom and pulled her closer. He wanted her to feel his arousal, for her to know how much he wanted her.

He would want her through eternity.

Dipping his head, he kissed her, long and hard and deep. So deep that she would have no choice but to forget the other man who'd kissed her tonight. He intended to seduce. To lose himself in every inch of her seductive body. He wanted to taste, to touch, to bury himself inside her.

Wanted her to feel this hot, searing, crazed need every bit as desperately as he.

Heat and desire rose in him while the taste of her seeped into him. His hands cupped her breasts, lingered there, then slid down her rib cage to her hips in a long, slow exploration, reacquainting himself with every curve, every slope of her body. In the moonlight, her dark eyes were hazy with desire. Against his chest, her heart pounded wildly and he felt the lonely ache he'd carried inside him for two years ease.

When her head fell back, he nuzzled her neck, careful to avoid the small bandage. Beneath his lips, he felt the unsteady thrum of her pulse.

Her breath hitched and a low, smoldering moan rose in her throat.

His mouth moved in an unhurried journey back to hers, then settled and dove in deep as his blood heated with the urgency to take. To give. To claim.

His fingers burrowed through her hair, loosening the rhinestone-studded comb and sending it clattering against the wood floor. Her arms went around his waist, her hands hesitating against the automatic at the small of his back.

Reaching around, he jerked the holstered weapon off his

waistband, laid it on the bureau beside the door. Already, her fingers were working on the buttons of his shirt.

"Let me," he said, his breathing abruptly heavy. He fought off his shoes. Tugged off his pants and shirt, leaving them lying on the floor as he guided her backward toward the bed.

When her thighs hit the silky white duvet, Claire clung to his shoulders with both hands while she kicked off her heels. Her breasts were tight, achy, her loins full. She kneaded her fingers across the muscled planes of his back, scraping and stroking until his flesh seemed to burn under her hands, and his muscles hardened like iron.

He found the zipper of her dress, and with one deft move managed both to unzip it and slide it down to her waist. She couldn't stop her body from shuddering when he lowered his head and began to devour the flesh above the black lace edge of her bra.

His tongue slid under, teasing and tasting while need clawed at her. With a flick of his fingers, he opened the front hook and let her breasts fill his hands.

"I've missed you, Claire," he murmured. "Missed this." His thumbs brushed across her nipples, budding them hard and tight. Desire flooded her veins like flame leaping along spilled gasoline.

Suddenly, she was falling backward onto the bed, falling through time and space until it seemed impossible that two years had passed since she'd made love with the man bracing himself over her. He tugged her dress down her thighs, tossed it away, then pulled off her black stockings in one rough, quick gesture.

Blood pounded in her head as the silver moonlight enhanced movements that knotted the muscles along his ribs and shoulders. His body was as magnificent as she remembered, all tanned and taut and leanly athletic. She reached, felt the sinewy strength in his thigh, then slid her hand higher, higher.

His eyes went dark. "You do much more of that, I can't promise to control myself."

"I don't want you to control yourself."

He pressed her into the mattress as his mouth came back to hers, restless, insistent. His hands molded, possessed, ratcheting her need up another tight notch. Her body writhing, she gripped his shoulders, holding on as the heat in her blood intensified, threatening to engulf her. Through a haze of desire, she saw nothing but his face, nothing but him. For her, Jackson Castle was all that existed.

She heard his breathing grow harsher as his hand slicked down her rib cage, across the flat plane of her stomach, then moved between her legs, cupping her. She nearly wept as each new lash of pleasure whipped through her. The air around her took on an edge, slicing into her lungs.

His fingers moved, driving her senses in a slow, familiar rhythm that was a part of her past and present, blending in the most exquisite sensations. Her body arched, her nails bit into his back as her system exploded, erupting in waves of annihilating heat. Light danced behind her eyes and she could do nothing but bury her face against his chest.

"You're the only woman I want," he said, his voice a low rasp as the rock-hard press of his body covered hers. "The only woman I'll ever want."

When he slipped inside her, her groan of pleasure echoed his own. She could count every beat of his pulse. This was the completeness she so desperately needed, that pure physical sensation that made her feel as if she had ceased to exist alone, and now existed as a part of him. She tried to speak, but no words came out.

With a throaty growl of her name, Jackson buried his face in her hair and followed her into deep, glorious pleasure.

Later, Jackson lay among the tangled sheets and listened to Claire's soft, steady breathing. She had fallen asleep with her arm thrown across his stomach and her head nestled on his shoulder. Her heartbeat had slowed to normal against his.

The silence of the night wove a web of intimacy around them.

The smell of her skin, the exotic fragrance of her perfume, the lingering scent of sex drifted through his senses. He had the taste of her in his mouth. He watched her in the pale wash of moonlight. Dark lashes fanned across her cheeks, still tinted with the lingering glow of pleasure. Her lips were parted slightly, her hot, sexy mouth swollen from his. She was so beautiful.

And this woman whom he loved beyond all reason didn't want the type of life he could give her.

Over the past two years, nothing had happened to bridge the gulf that existed between them. Their lifestyles hadn't meshed before. They still didn't.

His fingers slid across her tousled hair that spilled like black silk across his arm and onto the snow-white pillowcase. Dammit, he didn't want to live his life meeting her from time-to-time in whatever country they could both manage to get to. He stroked a fingertip along her shoulder, felt the silky skin, slim bones. He leaned, pressed a kiss against her temple.

She didn't stir.

Still, he wanted her back. And having her in his life in brief spaces was better than what he'd been living with. But he didn't know if he could settle for that, didn't know if she could. And if either of them couldn't—or wouldn't—what then?

He shifted his gaze and stared up at the shadowy ceiling while a sense of dread tightened his chest. Claire wasn't the only thing he stood to lose. The job that was so much a part of him was also at risk. Even now, when he let himself think about the suspension, he felt a faint, uncomfortable tug of panic. He knew it wasn't just due to the fact he had no idea if he could give up his nomadic lifestyle and settle down in one spot. Losing his job would effectively shut the door on his chances of finding out if his suspicions were right—that Ryker had teamed with Kaddur to carry out the bombing in Barcelona that killed his twin.

He had stood over Garrett's grave and vowed to avenge his death, aware that it could take months, even years, to do so. Knowing the risks involved, it would be less than fair to ask Claire to put her life on hold and wait for him.

Jackson eased out a breath. He needed to think long and hard about everything.

He was still mulling matters over when he shifted carefully, pulled Claire closer and slid into sleep.

Chapter 11

The following evening, Claire, Liz and Allie gathered for a girls-only session in the plush dressing room at the back of Silk & Secrets. Faint wisps of lavender haunted the air, along with the scent of the rain that had swept in an hour ago.

"So, you and the yummy fed did the hot-sheet samba last night?" Liz asked around a bite of chocolate cherry ice cream. The question was accompanied by a crash of thunder that reverberated through the sturdy brick building.

"That's not exactly the way I would describe our... activities, but you definitely got the drift," Claire said.

Curled into one corner of a powder-pink love seat, Claire regarded her friend skooched down in a plush up-holstered chair. Dressed in black capri pants and a red halter top, Liz wore her long, coppery hair loose. Her sun-browned legs were slung over one arm of the chair and a bowl brimming with ice cream was propped on her flat stomach. The sole evidence of her profession was the holstered automatic lying on the glass coffee table. Earlier, when Jackson had escorted Claire from her building next door through a mix of wind and slanting rain, Liz had assured him she would keep the weapon within arm's reach.

"Liz is just being her usual romantic self," Allie observed from the other end of the love seat where she'd curled up after kicking off her Manolo Blahniks. "And, Claire, no matter how you describe what you and Jackson did, in my opinion it's wonderful. Just thinking about former lovers who find their way back to each other has me melting faster than this decadent ice cream."

Liz arched a coppery brow. "This coming from a woman whose motto is: once I'm done with a man, there's no going back."

"Because I've never met one who was worth going back for." Allie licked a dollop of cherry off her spoon. Having attended a day-long board meeting of her family's investment empire, she was still dressed in a black Chanel suit and snow-white pearls. With her blond hair slicked back and secured by a diamond clip, she looked like she was worth millions, which she was.

"Claire has apparently decided that a certain solid, muscled stretch of good-looking man is worth going back for," Allie added.

"Being with Jackson again was wonderful," Claire

agreed while rain hammered the building's roof and windows.

Just thinking about the sensual feel of Jackson's hands slicking across her heated flesh, of every inch of his iron-hard body against hers put a tug of lust inside her. Still, a dull ache in her heart had her jabbing her spoon at her own ice cream. "Wonderful, and probably a huge mistake."

"Uh-oh," Liz said. "Why a mistake?"

"History. Things didn't work for Jackson and me before. There's no reason to think they will now." For Claire, it was the first time she'd put into words the thoughts that had plagued her since she'd wakened that morning, snuggled in Jackson's arms. Already she could feel the soft fingers of hopelessness plucking at her.

"You've spent two years apart," Allie pointed out. "All that time didn't kill what you feel for each other. Surely you can figure out some way to stay together and be happy."

"Speaking of staying together, I had to call your Jackson today," Liz said. "He told me his boss suspended him because he refused a direct order to leave you while his rogue ex-partner's on the loose. Sounds to me like Castle has already taken a long step toward staying here."

"He did?" Allie had gone stock-still, her cherry-chocolate-heaped spoon halfway between her bowl and her mouth. "Jackson refused to leave Claire?"

Wordlessly, Claire took a bite of ice cream. Although Jackson had told her last night about his suspension, she still felt a bump under her heart, and a quickening of her pulse over the fact he'd put her before the job that meant so much to him.

"Yep," Liz said. "I actually heard it first from Tom Iverson from Homeland Security. I ran into him today at an anti-terrorism workshop at the National Memorial Institute. I stopped him in the hall to see if there'd been any more reports of Ryker using his government credit card."

"Have there been?" Thunder cracked and sent an answering jolt into Claire's stomach. Each day that passed with the threat of Frank Ryker hanging over her heightened the sense of dread that kept her stomach knotted.

"There's been no activity on the G-card account since Ryker—or whoever has the card—used it a couple of days ago in northern Nevada," Liz said. "Looks to me like Ryker dropped off the radar, just like Castle predicted."

A twinge of icy premonition drifted up Claire's spine. "The other part of Jackson's prediction was that Ryker would head here."

"It's possible." Liz's gaze flicked to her holstered automatic on the table. "Which makes me breathe a lot easier over the fact that Castle bucked his boss to stay with you."

"That is so totally romantic," Allie said, and indulged in a sigh. "Claire, a man doesn't put his job on the line for a woman unless he's in love."

"Love isn't enough, Al. Jackson and I were in love two years ago, but that didn't solve our problems." If she allowed it, Claire knew she would find herself helplessly sucked in by Jackson having risked his job to stay with her. And then she'd be in danger of losing even more of her heart to him.

What she needed to do was *protect* her heart, not open it to more pain.

"Jackson feels responsible because he's the reason Ryker has targeted me," Claire said. "But when that threat is over, Jackson will leave, no matter his feelings for me."

"What if he gets fired?" Allie asked.

"He hunts terrorists and other bad guys for a living, and he's good at it. Jackson won't have a problem finding a similar job with another agency." Claire stabbed her fingers through her hair. "There's no way he can be happy tied to one place."

Liz pursed her mouth. "Sounds to me like he's tied to one woman."

"And people change," Allie pointed out, her voice almost obscured by another cannon shot of thunder. "You have to take that into account. Jackson might change."

"I haven't changed," Claire said. "No matter how I feel about Jackson, I won't give up the home and business I've wanted all my life. *I can't.* I'm sure that deep down he knows he'll be leaving here soon."

She swallowed hard while a finger of fear touched her heart. "And it isn't just because of some ingrained need to be on the move. The other day, before Jackson got suspended, I heard him talking to his boss on the phone about Hassan Kaddur."

"Who?" Allie asked.

"The terrorist Ryker sold blank U.S. passports to so he could pay for his daughter's heart transplant. Jackson suspects Kaddur's followers staged the Barcelona bombing that killed Jackson's twin brother. Jackson told his boss that if he ever got proof that Kaddur was involved, he would get him, no matter if it took him the rest of his life."

"That's some heavy-duty revenge," Liz said.

"And I know Jackson well enough to believe he'll never give up."

Because her throat had gone tight, Claire looked at Liz and changed the subject. "So, why did you call Jackson today?"

"Two reasons. I wanted to find out if he'd had a chance to talk to Adam Navarro at the museum last night. Castle said that Navarro brought up the subject of Charles's murder, and seemed surprised about the boxes of Spanish legal documents getting stolen from Charles's RV after he was murdered. Navarro freely admitted that he collects those types of documents so he can compile the Navarro family history."

"Sounds reasonable." Allie took another bite of ice cream. "Is there anything that connects the museum curator to the guy who murdered Charles and Silas and attacked Claire?"

"Not at this point," Liz advised. "The second reason I called Castle was to tell him I still haven't been able to get a judge to sign my court order to unseal Ike Bolton's juvie record. No matter that Bolton killed two men, then held a knife to Claire's throat, the judge wants to make sure I don't step on Bolton's rights."

Claire sat her empty bowl on the coffee table. "Didn't you say that unsealing the records might be the only way to find out about Bolton's relatives and former associates? And from those names there might be a lead to whoever sent him here for the paper he demanded I give him?"

"That sums it up," Liz said.

"I don't get it," Allie said. "Bolton murdered two men, and who knows what he'd have done to Claire if Jackson hadn't been here? Why should Bolton's rights matter, especially since he's dead?"

"As far as I'm concerned, the murderous scuzzball doesn't have any rights," Liz said. "But then I have to *act* like I think he does or I won't get anywhere with the bleeding-heart judge I have to deal with."

"Lovely," Allie said. "Has anyone told you there are aspects of your job that suck?"

"*I've* told myself that. But I'd much rather haul in do-wrongs than kowtow to rich, spoiled women who'd get a case of the vapors if they wore anything but your expensive silk skivvies."

"You'll find out just how sexy my skivvies make a woman feel when you're wearing what I've designed for your wedding night."

Allie's mouth formed a smug curve as she swept a hand in the direction of her drafting table where snippets of bright silk and delicate lace lay amid sketches of negligees, robes and bustiers. "Trust me, Liz, you won't have my gorgeous creation on for long after Andrew gets an eyeful."

Angling her chin, Liz downed another bite of ice cream. "Okay, you have a point. Just the thought of getting your sexy lingerie ripped off me by my hot new husband shifts my motor into overdrive."

"There's the romantic in you coming out again," Allie said dryly, then looked at Claire, her gaze softening. "What about you?"

"What about me?"

"Are you going to need some of my designs for a honeymoon, after all?"

All day, Claire had been thinking about what her future held. Despite the warnings and lectures to herself against it, she had fallen in love with Jackson again. Which made no sense, because the past had taught her there was no compromise that could make them both happy. He was too restless to settle down in one place and try to build a life with her. He would always be leaving, looking for something that she couldn't give him. Granted, he wanted her now, even needed her, but Jackson Castle would always be a leaver.

And she had dug in deep with her home and her shop and she wasn't going anywhere. Damn sure wouldn't let herself wind up like her mother, futilely chasing men and an elusive happiness from one place to another, then living…and dying in the back of a rusted van in an alcoholic haze.

"Better not count on my needing any of your honeymoon lingerie, Al," Claire said. "My marrying Jackson just isn't in the cards."

"But you'll spend time together when you can, right?" Allie asked. "Jackson can come back here, and you can hire an assistant to work in the shop so you can go meet him from time to time. I mean, for what's between you to have lasted this long, it must be hot and burning. Strong enough to last a lifetime."

A lifetime, Claire thought, as the vision popped into her head of herself waiting over a handful of decades for Jackson to reappear in her life for day-or-week spurts.

Always waiting.

God help her, she didn't think she could do that. Didn't think she could *let* herself do that.

The rain continued throughout the night and into early morning. Claire drifted awake in Jackson's arms. She listened to the water whispering down a drainpipe and thought about last night's conversation with Allie and Liz.

As much as she wanted Jackson, she also wanted a life with a husband who was home more than he was gone. And she wanted a father for her children who could be counted on to be around to help raise them, instead of off chasing enemies of the United States all over the globe.

As much as she wanted him to be, she knew that Jackson Castle was not the man for the job. And she was not the woman who could enrich his life and make him happy.

Maybe this time, she thought. Maybe his leaving this time would chase his memory back to where it belonged—securely in the past. Then she would do whatever it took to move on.

With a dark mire of sadness pulling at her, Claire pressed a kiss to his shoulder. Soundlessly, she slid from his arms and padded out of the bedroom.

"Yes, Mrs. DiCarlo, the Venetian glass bowls you saw in the shop are still available."

With the phone cradled between her shoulder and ear, Claire sat on the long-legged stool behind the shop's main counter and slid an order pad out of a drawer. She hoped the frisson of excitement she felt over her longtime customer asking about two of the most expensive items currently in Home Treasures' inventory didn't sound in her voice.

"Wonderful," Mrs. DiCarlo's voice boomed across the line. "My daughter, Olivia, hasn't stopped talking about the bowls since we left your shop. As I mentioned, she's a newlywed, and the bowls are too expensive for her budget. Not mine. Can you charge them to the credit card I used the other day? And gift wrap the package before you ship it to her in Florida?"

"Of course," Claire said.

"While you're at it, why don't you include the largest of the Rapallo lace tablecloths in with the bowls?"

"I'll be happy to."

"Also, Claire, I'd like you to hold the pair of Louis XV silver wine coolers you showed me. My husband and I are moving into our new home next week, and I think the coolers might look perfect in the area of the foyer you and I talked about. I'll have my decorator come by and look at them to make sure they'll work there."

"I'll hold them as long as you need me to."

Minutes later, Claire had the order and shipping information jotted on the pad. "Holy moly," she murmured after ending the call.

She glanced out the wide front window to the rain pouring down from low, gunmetal-gray clouds. Knowing it would be a miracle if any customers came in during the deluge, she reached under the counter. After nudging aside the small wooden chest sprouting dried sunflowers and baby's breath that she'd relocated onto the counter the previous day, she had the drawings she'd commissioned rolled out in front of her.

"Planning on having something built?"

Claire looked up with a start. As usual, Jackson had approached the counter as silently as a whisper.

"Not built, remodeled," she answered, as she looked back at the drawings. "But until a few minutes ago, doing so was more of a far-off dream than reality."

Jackson leaned his forearms on the counter. He looked rough and dangerous dressed all in black, his dark hair tousled and day-old stubble shadowing his jaw. She realized that in the time he'd been in Oklahoma City, the paper-thin scar that sliced through his left eyebrow had healed enough to lose all redness.

"What happened a few minutes ago?" he asked.

The incredible scent of musky aftershave and potent male surrounded her. Aroused her. *Keep your mind on the subject at hand,* she told herself.

"Do you remember the two women who came into the shop the day Liz was here talking to us? They were interested in lace tablecloths and doorstops."

"The mother-and-daughter team."

"Mrs. DiCarlo—the mother—just called. She ordered two Venetian-glass bowls and a tablecloth for her daughter. She also put two solid-silver wine coolers on hold for herself."

Jackson glanced down at the drawing rolled out on top of the glass counter. "I take it DiCarlo's order makes your bank account flush enough to remodel something?"

"Expand and remodel. About six months ago, the

woman who rents the space next door for her candle shop told me she and her husband were moving out of state and she wasn't going to renew her lease. I've been beefing up my savings for quite a while, so I had an architect draw up plans to expand Home Treasures into that space. I didn't think I'd have enough saved to be able to swing the expansion this soon, but if Mrs. DiCarlo adds the wine coolers to what she purchased today, that should put me over the top."

As Claire talked, Jackson studied her. Over the past two years he had gotten used to waking up without her. But this morning he had found himself alone in her bed with her subtle scent all around him, and he had felt the loss like a backhanded slap. Now, seeing the way her brown eyes lit with excitement and her skin glowed as she talked about expanding her shop left no doubt in his mind how committed she was to her business. So committed to staying in one place, he thought, that she might not be as interested as he in a long-term reconciliation.

His eyes narrowed as he shifted his gaze out the window to the wind-driven rain coming down in diagonal sweeps. He'd lost Claire once. He wasn't about to let that happen again. But, dammit, he didn't want her in snatches of day-or-week segments. He wanted her in his life full-time.

How the hell could he pull that off so they both had what they needed? The uncertainty of being able to manage that notched his frustration a degree higher. Months after she'd left him, he'd talked his boss into taking him out of the field and assigning him to a desk. Jackson had thought if he could handle that, *deal with it* and stay in one place, then maybe there would be a chance for himself and Claire.

But the time he'd spent in the restricting, confining cubicle had convinced him that hell itself had more pleasantries to offer. So he'd stayed away. Tried to forget her. Failed at making himself stop loving her.

Claire shoved her dark hair behind her shoulders. "My next step is to call the owner of the building next door to see if he's interested in selling."

"Selling, not leasing?"

"If I can buy the entire building, I could convert the second floor into an apartment to rent out. That would bring in additional income for me." She furrowed her forehead in thought. "*If* the building is for sale, then the next step is to have it checked. See if the foundation is strong. The roof sound."

Jackson studied the drawing. It was so much more than just an architect's sketch. It was a symbol that Claire intended to dig in deeper, put down more roots. Stay put.

"Claire." He spoke her name quietly as he settled his right hand over hers. "I was disappointed this morning when I woke up and you were gone."

Her eyes slid away from his. "I woke up early and couldn't go back to sleep. I didn't want to disturb you."

"I wish you had." He stroked his thumb over her knuckles, thinking about what she had told him after her self-defense lesson when things got hot and heavy between them. "I don't want you to regret last night. As far as I'm concerned, it's the farthest thing there is from a one-night stand."

Emotion flicked over her face. "I don't have any regrets. I know our making love meant as much to you as it did to me."

"Then how about we talk about where we go from here?"

"You mean after Ryker's no longer a threat and you leave?"

"I didn't say I was leaving. Right now it's up in the air whether I have a job to go back to."

She looked at him steadily. "If you're not working for the State Department, you'll find something else that keeps you on the move. I know you can't stay here with me full-time, any more than I can go with you."

Just hearing her say the words knotted his gut. "There's got to be some middle ground." He tightened his hand on hers. "Dammit, Claire, I want you in my life."

She reached up, cupped his cheek against her palm. "And I want you in mine."

"Then come with me when I leave."

"Come with me," she repeated, "and sit around some hotel room on the other side of the world while you hunt Hassan Kaddur and other people like him?"

"Kaddur and the members of his terrorist cell have murdered hundreds of people."

"Including Garrett. How many years of your life are you willing to give to hunting Kaddur?"

"Right now, no one in law enforcement knows where Kaddur is. My going after him isn't an option until we get intel about his location. If we ever do."

Claire closed her eyes for an instant. "Jackson, aren't you just a little bit afraid?"

"Damn right I am. I'm afraid of losing you again."

"What if I were to come with you, and it's like it was before?"

"There were a lot of good things about before."

"At first, yes. Not at the end when I realized that life on the road with you meant not seeing you the majority of the time. I lost count of how many hours—days—I spent alone, wondering if you were alive or dead. Maybe you've forgotten some of our arguments, but I haven't."

He looked away, shoved a hand through his hair. "I haven't forgotten anything," he said, his voice quiet. "And you're right. Things weren't good at the end."

"I've given us a lot of thought. Tried to figure out how we can stay together and both be happy."

"Come up with any ideas?"

"No." She let her hand drop from his cheek, then she squared her shoulders. "I'm beginning to think that the only way we can be a part of each other's lives, is to not *live* each other's lives."

He recognized withdrawal when it smacked him in the face, but he wasn't going to acknowledge it. Wasn't going to let her get away again. If he had to settle for brief snatches of her time, he would.

"Then I guess we have to settle for seeing each other as often as we can," he said evenly. "Make time to meet when I'm between assignments and you can get someone to mind the shop."

Her gaze stayed locked with his, her eyes bleak. "That's just it, Jackson. I don't know if I want to settle for that. I don't know if I *can*."

Just then, the shop's door swung open, emitting a sweep of rain-cool air along with a man and a woman, drenched to the teeth. Claire slid off the stool, moved around the counter and hustled the couple in with an accompanying welcome.

"Can't believe we're out shopping in this storm," the man grumbled while Claire hung their dripping raincoats on pegs above a wicker basket filled with water-absorbing paper.

"Hush, Harry," the woman said. "The open house starts at noon and we can't go without a gift."

"Help yourself to coffee," Claire said, inclining her head toward the small linen-covered table that held a silver coffee service. "You're welcome to browse. Let me know if I can help you with anything."

His frustration mounting, Jackson headed toward the rear of the shop. He was very aware he was caught between what he was and what he wanted, and he had no idea what to do about it. No idea if there was anything he *could* do about it.

From the other side of Reunion Square, Frank Ryker stood in the shadowed doorway of an empty building and slid his powerful binoculars into the pocket of his trench coat.

He was aware of the slight trembling in his hands.

He'd felt overwhelmingly sick when he first spotted Jackson Castle standing at the counter in the quaint antique shop. The man he'd once considered a friend had sent to the safe house the MSD team that had killed his wife and his daughter. *They* hadn't caused any trouble. They hadn't done *anything* to deserve getting gunned down.

All he and his wife had wanted was to buy a heart for their ill daughter so she could live. They'd been desperate to save Emily.

Thinking about all he had lost filled Ryker's mouth with a bitter, steely taste. In a cold sweat, he shoved his personal nightmare aside.

He had expected the obvious trail of G-card purchases he'd made toward the west coast would get Castle assigned as the primary agent on his trail. Yet, here he was in Oklahoma City at the side of his former lady love. Ryker had no idea how Castle had figured out he would target Claire Munroe. But it was just as well he had. After all, Ryker had planned on tracking down his former partner after he killed the woman.

So convenient, he thought, when one's prey stepped willingly into the trap. Still, it was a complication. And complications required careful thought and planning before one acted.

He would wait, Ryker decided, his gaze locked on the shop's front window. Wait, and time his entrance for when he had the most chance of success.

Chapter 12

By late afternoon, the rain had pared down to a steady drizzle. Claire kept scented votives lit throughout the shop and set out a pot of tea and a platter of scones. The homey atmosphere and comfort food prompted the customers that braved the damp weather to stay in the shop for lengthy browsing sessions.

Claire had to fight a smile when she thought about the hefty sales she'd rung up throughout the rainy day.

"From what I've seen, the shop's doing a landmark business," Jackson said when he appeared a half hour before closing time. He'd positioned himself with a hip against the front counter, standing with his arms crossed, his body apparently relaxed. Yet every few seconds his intent gaze focused like a laser out the front window.

Although she'd been so busy that she'd caught only a few glimpses of him during the day, Claire knew he had been close by, watching for any sign of Frank Ryker.

Her gaze tracked Jackson's toward the window. Reunion Square's lush green grass and wooden benches were deserted in the steady, dismal drizzle. She felt a prick of apprehension over Jackson's prediction that the rogue federal agent might be on his way to harm her. Jackson was here, she reminded herself. Standing only inches away, ready, willing and able to protect her.

"Sales have been very good today," she agreed, forcing back thoughts of Ryker.

She shifted her attention to the far side of the shop where a redhead and a blonde decked out in designer jeans and slinky blouses nibbled on scones while checking out a circa 1860 rose-strewn French screen. "I'm glad I thought to have the bakery deliver the scones."

"You're good at this," Jackson said, his blue eyes now locked with intensity on her face.

"At ordering bakery items?"

"At everything," he said quietly. "When we first met, you talked about buying this shop one day from Charles. I couldn't picture you doing that. Didn't even try because I knew it meant you'd come back here to stay. I disliked just the thought of that because I wanted you with me."

His words had her heart sticking in her throat. "And I wanted to be with you."

He leaned in. "Claire, we're going to find a way to make us work," he said as softly as a lover whispering endearments. "We have to."

"Excuse me," the blond customer said, craning her head in Claire's direction. "I've got some questions about this screen."

"I'll be right with you." Letting out a shaky breath, Claire looked back at Jackson. "We'll have to talk later."

"I'm counting on it."

Leaving Jackson at the counter, she threaded her way toward the opposite side of the shop. While she moved, she realized she still harbored a small burst of hope that somehow, someway, they might find a way to merge their lives.

Think about that later, she told herself as she neared the two women. "How can I help you?"

The blonde had long, wavy hair, beautifully finished makeup and a beaming smile. "I'm hoping you and I can work a deal for this gorgeous screen that won't hitch my husband's blood pressure too high."

"Let's see what we can do."

Frank Ryker shoved up the cuff of his raincoat and checked his watch. It was nearly closing time. When the hell were those two women going to leave?

He had moved around all day, surveilling the shop from various vantage points, using the camouflaging drizzle to his advantage while he studied the brick building. If Castle had been with the woman for any length of time, he would have installed security measures in and around the structure. Because he had trained Castle, Ryker had a good idea of what those would be.

The only time things got dicey during the day was when Castle left the shop and walked the square's perimeter.

Ryker knew that his shaved head, heavy whiskers and colored contacts would fool just about everyone who knew him...except his former partner. His instincts were too good. Too honed.

Ryker smiled to himself, the unpleasant smile of a hunter. *He* was good, too. And because he didn't want to take a chance at being spotted while his protégé was out and about, Ryker had abandoned his surveillance and taken refuge in a diner three blocks away.

After all, it wasn't Jackson Castle he planned to get his hands on first. It was his woman.

When the door to the shop swung open, Ryker held his breath until the blonde and redhead exited. He re-checked his watch, raised the binoculars. It was almost closing time. Claire Munroe and Castle were the only people left in the shop.

Tugging down the brim of his baseball cap, Ryker headed around the fringe of Reunion Square. When he neared Home Treasures, he pulled the jammer out of his raincoat pocket and aimed it at the security camera on the upper corner of the brick building.

He paused at one side of the door, canted his body so he could peer through the glass. As he expected, Castle pulled his cell phone off his belt and checked the display. After speaking to Munroe, he headed up the stairs at the rear of the shop.

Ryker waited ten seconds before he eased the door open.

* * *

He didn't want to spend time now running diagnostics on a security camera, Jackson thought as he bounded up the stairs. He wanted to talk to Claire. Get things settled.

Figure out where they went from here.

But the alert that had sounded moments ago on his cell phone indicated the surveillance camera on the northwest corner of the building had gone off-line. The other cameras, motion detectors and sensors placed around the building were still operating, so he didn't have a solid reason to suspect the problem with the camera aimed toward Reunion Square was due to anything other than the damp weather. Or maybe a sudden glitch with the software or hardware.

He swung open the door of the second-floor storage room where several monitors glowed with shots of the exterior around the building. One monitor displayed what looked like a snowstorm. Scowling, Jackson stepped to a desk, tapped instructions into a keyboard.

Just as scrolling lines of text replaced the snowstorm on the monitor, his cell phone rang. He lifted a brow when he saw his boss's number on the display.

Wondering if a decision had been made on the fate of his job, Jackson answered the call.

"You were right." His boss's voice was abrupt and to the point.

"About?"

"Ryker. A couple of nights ago, a drunk in a Texas Panhandle watering hole picked a fight with a stranger. When the drunk tried to take a swing, the stranger kicked his leg out from under him. The drunk fell, smashed his head against a table. The blow killed him. By the time the cops arrived, the stranger was long gone. The cops dusted his beer bottle for prints. They were Ryker's."

Jackson's grip tightened on the phone. "He's on his way to Oklahoma."

"Looks like."

"Or already here."

"Anything happen that makes you think he is?"

Jackson stared at the text scrolling on the monitor. "I'll get back to you."

With dread clamping a vise on his chest, he slid his automatic from the holster at the small of his back. Soundlessly, he moved out of the storage room.

At the top of the stairs he paused, listened. The silence was broken only by the low hum of the air-conditioning. Which in itself wasn't anything to be concerned about. Claire had been on her way to lock the shop's front door and flip the open sign to closed when he came upstairs. As far as he knew, there was no one downstairs, but her.

Nothing about the stillness set off Jackson's cop vibes. Even so, a deep intuitive sense of unease swept through him.

Claire. He needed to get to Claire.

Moving as silently as a jaguar stalking prey, he thumbed off the automatic's safety. Keeping his back to the wall, he eased down the staircase, pausing on the bottom step.

From where he stood he had a view of about a quarter

of the shop. His gaze swept over china, silver and the myriad of antiques displayed on racks, tables and cabinets. Nothing looked out of place.

He stood unmoving, adrenaline running, listening while the scent of cinnamon and vanilla filled his lungs. He wanted to call out for Claire, but an instinctual wariness kept him silent.

Gun aimed, he peered around the corner. His breath caught when he spotted Claire. She was sitting with her back to him, in the high-backed, ornate wooden chair he'd always figured had come out of some English mansion. He couldn't see her face, but her head listed unnaturally to one side. Beside the chair was a linen-draped table where votive candles flickered.

Ryker. Jackson couldn't see his former partner, couldn't hear him, but the tightness in his gut told him Ryker was nearby.

Was Claire still alive? He didn't dare give his position away by calling to her.

A sick dread pounded in Jackson's brain. Training battered with the urge to rush to her, but he held himself back. He wouldn't be any good to Claire if he stepped into a trap.

Still, he couldn't just stand there all day, his hands gripped on his automatic. He had to move, *needed* to get to Claire.

He eased forward, step by step. Inch by inch the interior of the shop came into view. All of Jackson's senses were on alert. He saw no sign of Ryker, heard nothing.

Yet, he sensed time was running out, ticking like a metronome in his head. In his gut.

He stepped fully around the corner, his gaze sweeping the shop's interior. He passed a hutch brimming with china, a credenza loaded with silver, a heavy tapestry that hung on a thick brass rod affixed to the wall.

At first, the mist that hit the side of his face was so light it almost didn't register. Instantly, dizziness swirled up from the floor. His eyes watered, his lungs burned. Jackson clumsily steadied himself against a table. His gun hand trembled. His legs began to shake, finally giving out.

The room spun and he fell into a roaring, buffeting darkness.

"Wake up, Claire. *Wake up.* I don't have all day."

Claire floated toward consciousness like a diver drifting up to the surface from the depths of the sea. Light flickered into what had been total blackness. As soon as she broke the surface, she wanted to go back down. Her eyes stung and watered; her lungs burned.

"Wake up."

When she managed to lift her head it lolled back, hitting something hard. Wood? She tried to raise her hands, but whatever was wrapped around her wrists prevented that.

Memory came back to her in a rush. The tall, bald man walking into Home Treasures at two minutes to closing time, saying his wife was shopping next door at Silk &

Secrets and he wanted to browse. His smile never reached his eyes as he shrugged out of his raincoat while wandering toward the counter where Claire had paused on her way to lock the shop's front door.

His hand sweeping up. Her spotting the small metal canister clenched in his fingers a second before the spray hit her face. She had opened her mouth to scream for Jackson, but fire ignited in her eyes and lungs, then her legs gave out and she fell into darkness.

"Get with the program, Claire."

Forcing her eyes open, she struggled to focus as she swept her gaze around. She was in the corner of the shop farthest away from the front door, sitting on the elegant sixteenth-century shield-back English Renaissance throne chair. *Tied* to the chair she realized, as she struggled against the braided silk cords that bound her wrists to the thick, carved arms.

"That's better." The bald man stepped into her range of view and leaned down, putting his face even with hers. "Do you know who I am?"

The haziness began to fade, and fear took its place. He looked nothing like the pictures she'd seen of Frank Ryker. His denim shirt and jeans hung loose on his tall frame, as if he'd lost weight. His head was shaved, his jaw stubbled and his eyes were empty. Dead eyes. It was like looking into the window of a vacant house.

A sick sense of dread pushed at the base of her throat and she swallowed convulsively. "Ryker."

"Excellent." He angled his chin. "We can skip the introductions and get down to business."

"Where…." She shook her head in an attempt to clear it. "Jackson. Where's Jackson?"

Ryker stepped back, swept his hand toward one side of the chair. "He's right here. When I first arrived and saw him with you, I was surprised. But one has to be flexible in times of emergency."

Oh, God. A bubble of panic rose in Claire's throat when she spotted Jackson on the floor. He was lying on his side with his back to her so she couldn't see his face. A crimson silk cord bound his hands behind him and there was a complete stillness about him that told her he was unconscious.

Or worse.

Not worse, she told herself. Ryker wouldn't have had a reason to tie Jackson's wrists together if he were dead. She could see no blood matting his hair, none on the wooden floor. If Ryker had used the same spray to knock out Jackson as he had her, Jackson might regain consciousness any moment.

When she renewed her struggles against the cords that bound her to the chair, Ryker's hand clamped on her chin, forcing her gaze back to his.

"I'm not sure how Castle figured out I would come after you, but it's convenient he did. Saves me from hunting him after I'm done with you."

She jerked futilely against the woven cords. With her wrists tied to the chair, she had no hope of using any of the lethal self-defense moves Jackson had taught her.

"Killing us won't bring your wife and daughter back," she said flatly.

As if a switch had been flipped, Ryker's eyes instantly blazed into hers, almost black with revenge. "Did he tell you he killed them? Did my former partner tell you he murdered my wife and child?"

Claire's heart slammed against her ribs. She took a deep, burning breath to try to control the adrenaline rushing through her system. Something told her that if she let her fear show that Ryker would feed on it.

"Jackson told me what *you* did that got your family killed."

"Lies," Ryker spat, his fingernails digging into her flesh. "My daughter was ill. All I did was to try to save Emily's life."

"By selling blank U.S. passports to a terrorist? And setting up your fellow agents?"

"I had no choice!" His fingers unclamped from Claire's chin. He stalked the short distance to a hutch filled with bone china, then whipped around to face her. "I needed money. Fast. Over a million dollars to buy a heart on the black market for Emily's transplant. To pay a surgeon. I wanted her to get well. *To live.*"

Ryker advanced on Claire, his hands fisted. "I would have sold my soul to the devil to save her."

The thick grief in his voice had Claire clamping down on a stir of pity. He may have acted out of his consuming love for his child, but what he had done was abhorrent.

"I'm sorry about your family," she said, keeping her gaze locked on Ryker's. "I'm also very sorry about Jackson's twin brother, Garrett. He was a good man who didn't deserve to die. You did that, didn't you? You set up the bombing in Barcelona that killed Garrett Castle."

"It was my idea, but I can't claim all the credit." Ryker looked down at her and smiled like a snake. "My business associate, Hassan Kaddur, ordered several of the extremists he controls to carry out the deed."

The mention of the terrorist whom Jackson suspected had orchestrated the bombing sent a chill up Claire's spine. Confirmation that Ryker had aligned himself with someone so darkly evil gave her no hope that there was enough good left in Ryker for him to spare her and Jackson's lives.

Watching her, Ryker tilted his head. "You've heard Kaddur's name." It wasn't a question. He looked at Jackson. "Which means Castle figured out I had something to do with his brother's death. And that Kaddur's faction orchestrated the bombing, even though they've never claimed responsibility."

"That's right," Claire said. "Everyone knows what you've become."

"I'll be sure to tell Kaddur how infamous he is when I meet with him in Istanbul."

Ryker stepped closer, held up two fingers in front of her face. "Garrett Castle is dead," he said and flicked down one finger. "Today I even the score by letting my former partner watch the woman he loves die, just as my wife and daughter did. After that, he's a dead man."

With Jackson in her peripheral vision, Claire saw his head move, then his fingers twitch. Her heart flipped over. The good news was he was regaining consciousness. As soon as he did, however, Ryker intended to kill them. She couldn't just sit there helpless and let it happen. Somehow, she had to divert Ryker's attention to give Jackson time to fully come to.

She curled her fingers into her palms so he wouldn't see them shaking. "Revenge never brings back what was lost."

"Perhaps not," Ryker agreed. "But it sure as hell helps balance the scales."

"So, you became a murderer. My handyman. Charles."

When Ryker furrowed his brow, she rushed on. She had to keep him occupied.

"What would your Emily think about you now?" Claire's blood pounded so hard in her ears, it was a wonder she could hear Ryker. "Do you think she would still look at you with the same love in her eyes if she knew you killed Garrett Castle? And that you plan on murdering two more people in cold blood?"

Instantly, the back of Ryker's hand delivered a mind-numbing blow against Claire's cheek. Her head slammed against the chair's wooden back; lights exploded before her eyes.

"Don't talk about Emily! Don't you even say her name!"

Despite the blinding pain in her head and the taste of blood in her mouth, Claire welcomed the blow. It had scooted the heavy chair sideways against the round, linen-covered table where several lighted votives sat. Keeping her head lowered, she shifted her gaze to the table. Next to it sat a French scrolled pedestal holding a delicate glass kerosene lamp.

At that instant, Jackson groaned. Ryker glanced at

him, then smiled at Claire. "Looks like it's showtime. I hope you're ready to die."

With fear drenching her skin, Claire put all her strength into rocking the chair sideways. Its heavy armrest slammed against the table, toppling it into the pedestal. The lamp crashed to the floor and shattered, spattering kerosene.

Ryker cursed when the fuel splashed the legs of his jeans. The lighted votives ignited the kerosene in a thunderous whoosh that lit the linen tablecloth and spread outward.

In the next instant, flames engulfed Ryker's jeans. Howling, he dropped to the floor and attempted to roll in the cramped space, crashing into displays and upending tables while trying to douse his flaming clothing.

"Jackson!" Claire shouted as she fought the silk cords that held her prisoner in the chair. "Jackson, wake up!"

Chapter 13

His vision blurred, lungs burning, Jackson lifted his head off the floor. In his half-lucid state, everything was fuzzy and disjointed. He couldn't think coherently. Couldn't move his arms.

He made a futile attempt at blinking his bleary vision into focus.

In a hazy flash of memory he saw himself easing down the stairs, automatic drawn. Spotting Claire in the carved wooden chair. Feeling an almost imperceptible spray hit his right cheek, then he'd dropped and blacked out.

Ryker.

"Jackson!"

Claire's scream blew away the last of the sticky

cobwebs in his brain. Blinking again, he realized his fuzzy vision wasn't due to injury, but smoke.

Thick, acrid smoke.

With his wrists bound behind him, Jackson used an elbow to lever into a sitting position.

And saw that one corner of the shop looked like an inferno. Adrenaline pumped through him like a drug, driving him to his knees, his feet.

The air was almost too hot to breathe. A few yards away, a river of fire flowed across the floor, flames licking greedily at wood, tablecloths and linens.

"Claire?" Disoriented, he spun, attempting to get his bearings through the smoke. "Claire, where are you?"

"Here!" she screamed over the roar of the fire that was devouring the tapestry hanging against the wall. "In the throne chair. I'm tied to it!"

Following the sound of her voice, Jackson plowed through the smoke, bumping into tables and displays. When he finally reached her, he saw that her wrists were tied to the chair's heavy wood arms. Whipping around, he used his bound hands to grope at one of the thick cords holding her captive.

"Where's Ryker?"

"In the fire." Claire coughed while Jackson's fingers worked the knot. "Somewhere in the fire."

The instant he freed her wrist, an almost inhuman scream split the air. Jackson jerked his head around. Through the billowing smoke, he saw Ryker, his legs engulfed in flame as he managed to stand and tried frantically to run, stumbling into a hutch, crashing over a table.

Jackson gritted his teeth while Claire used her free hand to grapple at the cord that bound his wrists. When he felt the knot loosen, he fought off the binding. Seconds later, he freed Claire's other wrist, pulled her out of the chair and into a crouch.

"Stay low, there's more air down here," he said around coughs. "Get outside. Call 9-1-1."

"I'm not leaving you in here!" Her voice sounded like a load of gravel.

A big part of Jackson wanted to drag her to safety and leave Ryker to the flames because of all he'd done, the people he'd killed. But Jackson had been partners with the man too long. He couldn't do it. "I've got to get Ryker."

"We'll both get him!" The sound of Claire's wracking coughs was almost consumed by the bellow of the fire.

Not wanting to waste precious seconds debating, Jackson gripped her arm. Blinded, lungs straining, he groped his way toward Ryker's screams through what felt like a living wall of smoke. Suddenly, it seemed to part and he spotted his former partner on the floor, the lower half of his body engulfed in flames.

"Use this!" Claire shoved what felt like a wool blanket into Jackson's arms. He began beating at Ryker's legs, finally extinguishing his burning clothes.

The sickening-sweet smell of burnt flesh seared into Jackson's lungs.

"Let's get him out," he shouted. The smoke had turned his voice as rough as pine bark.

Jackson grabbed Ryker by one shoulder, Claire the

other, and together they dragged the rogue agent away from the flames and suffocating smoke.

They stumbled outside into the early evening drizzle. As if by silent agreement, neither stopped until they had Ryker across the street onto the grassy square where the air was almost free of smoke.

Claire dropped to her knees first, then Jackson. The coughing fit that seized her sounded like it might shatter a rib.

Pulling in deep breaths of the clean, damp air, Jackson used a forearm to wipe soot from his watering eyes. He waited until Claire caught her breath, then he reached for her. Her face was streaked with black, her white blouse dark gray from the smoke. "Are you okay? Baby, are you okay?"

"Yes." Tears streamed down her face, leaving a path through the soot. "I thought…" Beneath his hands, he felt her shudder. "I thought we were going to die."

"We're okay now." The wail of sirens pierced the air as he pulled her close. "We're okay."

"Is Ryker dead?" Her words came out in a heavy rasp against his shoulder.

Jackson shifted his gaze. Frank Ryker lay on his back, his face and shaved head blackened by soot, his eyes staring glassily upward.

"Yeah, he's dead." Despite what Ryker had done, Jackson couldn't help but feel remorse over the man to whom he'd once felt so close.

Claire eased her head back and stared across the street. "Oh, Jackson, my shop. My home." Her tears turned to racking sobs.

"We'll fix it." He stroked her hair away from her face. "We'll fix everything," he whispered and tightened his arm around her.

While the sirens grew louder, Jackson watched the dark smoke billow out the door while guilt settled in his stomach like a huge, jagged rock.

For Claire, it seemed like hours between the time she and Jackson dragged Ryker's dead weight out of the shop and the arrival of the firefighters from the downtown station two blocks away.

In reality, she was still on her knees, hacking smoke out of her lungs when the siren-blaring fire truck tore into view. At the same time, Allie dashed out of Silk & Secrets wearing an electric-blue cocktail dress and stilettos. Still clutching the phone she'd used to call 9-1-1 when she'd smelled smoke, Allie grasped Claire's hand while firefighters in full bunker gear rushed into Home Treasures, dragging lines of hoses.

Summoned by a phone call from Jackson, Liz arrived in official cop capacity. After learning the dead man lying at the edge of Reunion Square was federal agent Frank Ryker, Liz notified Tom Iverson from the Homeland Security Office, who contacted the State Department.

Looking back, Claire didn't remember many details about the trip to the E.R. where she and Jackson were checked out. Or about the hours spent in separate rooms at police headquarters while Liz and Tom Iverson took their statements.

When the interviews were over, Liz handed Claire

keys to her loft apartment at the Montgomery. Saying she would bunk at her fiancé's place, Liz told Claire and Jackson they had the use of the loft for as long as they needed. Claire hadn't argued. By then she was so physically and emotionally spent there was no way she could deal with returning to her building and facing the fire's devastation. Lying in Jackson's arms that night in Liz's big iron bed, Claire had tried to convince herself she was imagining the worst, that the damage to her home and business wouldn't seem so bad the following morning.

She'd been dead wrong.

Now, standing in the center of her shop, she stared at the area where the fire had started, while the smell of doused ash, sour and acrid, left a taste in her mouth. That section of the shop looked as dark as a coal mine and a heavy layer of soot covered everything.

The massive throne chair Ryker had lashed her to was nothing more than a blackened pile of cinders.

Claire blinked, dangerously close to tears. She had felt weepy since the instant she and Jackson walked into the building an hour ago. Although he'd offered to help start the inventory of damaged stock the insurance adjuster needed, Claire had suggested he go upstairs and check the security equipment in the storage room for damage. Right now, she needed to be alone, to try to get her emotions under some sort of control.

Which wasn't going to be easy when just walking crushed broken china and crystal to a sugary consistency beneath her sturdy work boots. The sound, a reminder of how many of her treasures were lost, made her shudder.

As did the smoky film that had turned the entire shop gray. The fire seemed to have leached the color out of everything and the burned area looked like a black-and-white photograph.

She thought vaguely about the paper Ike Bolton had demanded while he held a knife to her throat. If the paper was actually hidden somewhere in the shop, it was possible it had been destroyed in the fire. She might never know the reason her handyman and Charles had been murdered.

Claire jammed her fingers into the back pockets of her jeans and shifted her mind to business. She knew she had a lot to be thankful for. The building and all its contents were fully insured. Hours before the fire, a shipping service had picked up the package with the Venetian glass bowls and Rapallo lace tablecloths that Mrs. DiCarlo had ordered for her daughter. And Claire had moved the pair of Louis XV silver wine coolers Mrs. DiCarlo had her eye on to the upstairs storage room. That, and her apartment, had suffered only smoke damage. A cleaning company had already picked up her area rugs, upholstered furniture, bedding and other items that reeked of smoke.

Downstairs was another matter. The burned area in the shop had to be gutted, and a portion of the ceiling and wood floor repaired before she would have any idea of when she could reopen for business. In the meantime, she had an inventory to compile.

She moved to the main counter at the front where the door stood open, allowing the stiff morning wind to whip fresh air inside the shop. She was digging through a drawer for a rag to clean off the counter when Jackson stepped into view. His white golf shirt and tan khakis sported streaks of soot.

"Don't tell me you already have all the security equipment checked," she said. "I'm just now getting ready to start the inventory."

"Claire, something's come up."

The unease in his voice had her looking up. Emotion, something like regret, only more complex, flickered briefly in his blue eyes.

The pull on her heart was immediate and devastating. She knew that look from their past—she had seen it several times after their relationship had turned shaky and Jackson was about to leave her again for yet another assignment.

Sliding the drawer closed, she tightened her fingers on the rag she'd retrieved. Hot tears burned in the back of her throat, but she'd be damned if she would cry. *That* she promised herself. "What's come up?" she asked quietly.

"My boss called a few minutes ago."

"I'll lay odds that since you were right about Ryker coming here, you've been reinstated."

"You'd win that bet." Jackson scrubbed a hand over his stubbled jaw. "The lab examined the numbers on the cell phone I found in the pocket of Ryker's raincoat. One number that shows up a couple of times belongs to an individual whom our intel currently puts in Istanbul."

"Which is where Ryker told me he would be meeting Hassan Kaddur."

"Right. Our intel people have picked up chatter about an upcoming meeting between war lords and Kaddur somewhere in Turkey. Until now, there's been no intel on the location of that meeting."

Because she didn't want Jackson to see that her churning emotions had turned her hands unsteady, Claire ran the rag over the top of the glass counter. "Someone knows the location now, I take it?" The cloth turned black from the soot, so she doubled it over and gave the counter another swipe. She had known Jackson would leave eventually. Of course she had known.

"Not exactly," he answered. "The number Ryker called a couple of times belongs to Kaddur's spiritual advisor. Our people have the guy under surveillance. It's well-known Kaddur doesn't make any decisions without his advisor's input, so it's almost certain he's in Istanbul to attend the meeting. All we have to do is follow him and wait for Kaddur to show."

"I take it you intend to be there, too?" Claire's stomach was knotted and her lungs felt tight. Had she honestly fooled herself into believing she could watch Jackson walk away again and feel nothing?

"I *have* to be there, Claire. Kaddur ordered his fanatics to blow up my brother and a lot of other people. I'm going to make sure the bastard doesn't get away."

Not trusting herself to meet Jackson's gaze, she lifted the small sea captain's chest from the edge of the counter and placed it in front of her. She was grateful one of the items in the last shipment Charles sent her had escaped the fire unscathed, but the baby's breath sprouting out of it was black with soot. It occurred to her that she had no idea who the potential buyer was that Charles had for the chest.

When she plucked out the first branch, Jackson's hand curled around her wrist. "Dammit, Claire, I don't want to leave you. Especially now when you've got so much to deal with."

Dragging in a breath, she dropped the baby's breath and forced herself to meet his gaze. "I understand."

"Kaddur first surfaced on the scene about five years ago, and this is the *first* righteous intel we've got on him. I may never get another chance at him."

"Jackson, I said I understand. It's your job to go after terrorists like Kaddur. I loved Garrett, too, and I want the people who killed him to pay."

Keeping his hand locked on her wrist, Jackson moved around the counter to stand in front of her.

"I'll be back here as soon as possible," he said, grazing his knuckles across her cheek. "We'll take time for ourselves then. Figure out how to work our lives so they mesh."

She had known for a long time there were places inside him that no one, no woman, could ever touch. Had known she would never be everything he needed. Understood that it was impossible for her to reach the part of him that lived for danger, the adrenaline rush. Jackson Castle was the type of man who had to feel his actions made a difference, and she didn't for one minute believe he could be happy and content settled in one place.

She gazed up into the blue eyes locked on her face. Even if he did come back, she knew in her heart it wouldn't be for long. He might deny it, but he would never make a real home with her, he simply didn't have it in him to do that. And she didn't have the emotional energy right now to argue the point with him.

What would be the use?

She forced her mouth to curve. "I've got plenty to keep me busy, no matter how long you're gone. The memorial service for Charles is next week, so I need to make calls to let people know. And if the owner of the building next door agrees to sell to me, I'll have to incorporate the store's expansion into the structural repairs that need to be done. I'll barely have time to breathe."

"You'll stay with Liz at her loft, right? I don't want you here alone at night as long as there are so many unanswered questions about Ike Bolton."

"Since the cleaning service has already hauled off my bed and couch, I don't have much choice but to stay at the Montgomery."

Claire's throat began to ache. Why did following one's heart cause so much pain? "When do you leave?"

"My flight takes off in two hours."

"You'd better get packed."

"Claire, I promise you—"

"Don't." The word came out in a thick whisper as she touched an unsteady finger to his lips. "This isn't the time for promises." Especially not from a man who could only give a portion of himself.

"All right." He turned her hand in his, pressed his mouth to the inside of her wrist where her pulse thrummed. "I'll save my promises for when I get back. And I *will* be back, Claire."

* * *

For the next few hours, Claire worked like a fiend. Firing up her laptop, she created a spreadsheet listing the stock destroyed in the fire. After e-mailing the list to her insurance agent, she left a message for the owner of the building next door, then called the contractor who'd done the remodeling when she'd bought her building from Charles. Keeping busy, she knew from past experience, was the one thing that would help hold back the image of Jackson walking away, duffel bag in hand.

God, how often in one lifetime was she supposed to watch the man she loved walk away?

Having moved back to the front counter where fresh air wafting through the open door helped dull the smoke smell, Claire massaged lemon oil into the small sea captain's chest. She wasn't going to cry, she told herself for the umpteenth time when her thoughts drifted to Jackson and her eyes began to sting. Dammit, she had shed all the tears she was going to over the man. Setting her jaw, Claire focused her polishing on the chest's short, knobby legs.

And yelped when a small drawer at the lower edge of the chest popped open.

She stood motionless, rag gripped in her fist, staring into the drawer at what looked like a single piece of paper.

Parchment, she amended when she slid it out and unfolded it.

The text was handwritten in Spanish and surrounded by an ornate border. Some sort of deed, Claire decided as she scanned the first paragraph. Then the second. Everything inside her went still when the name *Navarro* jumped out at her.

Her gaze scrolled downward to the two signatures scrawled in heavy, black ink. The first belonged to Miguel Navarro. The second to General Antonio López de Santa Anna.

"Holy cow," Claire whispered, her eyes going wide. She didn't remember enough of her high-school Spanish to figure out what sort of property had been deeded to Miguel Navarro, but the signature of the general whose troops had defeated the defenders of the Alamo automatically lent the document value.

With the Navarro name involved, she had no doubt that Charles had hidden the deed in the chest he'd purchased at the California estate sale. After all, he'd spent years buying up Spanish legal documents solely to keep them out of Adam Navarro's clutches.

Was *this* the paper Ike Bolton had threatened to cut her throat over? The question brought all of Claire's nerves swimming to the surface. If the parchment was what Bolton had wanted, it was highly possible a connection existed between the museum curator and the man who had murdered Silas Smith and Charles.

Her mouth dry, Claire laid the parchment on the counter, grabbed her cell phone and dialed Liz's number.

When the call went to voice mail, impatience burned through her. "Liz, it's Claire. There's a hidden drawer in the small chest that Charles shipped here. I may have just found what Ike Bolton was looking for." She hesitated, then added, "Jackson left for the Middle East, so I hope you don't mind having me for a roommate at your loft for a while."

Claire laid her phone aside, picked up the parchment and studied the flowing black script, wishing she could interpret the Spanish. It took a moment for her to become aware of a slight tingle across her flesh. She glanced up, and felt her heart hitch.

For a moment she was too stunned to speak. She hadn't heard Adam Navarro step through the open door. Hadn't heard him close it behind him.

Her pulse hammered as she folded the parchment. Had he heard the message she left Liz?

"Mr. Navarro." She forced a smile. "I didn't hear you come in."

"I know." He was dressed in a dark suit, starched white shirt and crimson tie. His left hand was in clear view, but his right was concealed in the pocket of his suit coat. "Your fire was the lead story on this morning's news. I had to come and see the damage for myself. You must be devastated."

"Yes." She slid the parchment into the back pocket of her jeans. "I'm still in shock." Her gaze flicked across his shoulder. "The smoke smell is so strong in here, I'd appreciate it if you would leave the door open."

"I prefer to keep it closed and locked. Claire, we seem to have a problem."

"Which is?"

"Business best discussed in private."

"Then it will have to wait. Mr. Castle had to run upstairs to get something, but he'll be down here in a minute."

"It's a talented man who can be here and on his way to the Middle East all at the same time."

The hope that her bluff would work slid through Claire's fingers like cold, dry sand. Navarro had clearly overheard her message to Liz.

"The shop's back room will do."

When he saw Claire's eyes cut toward the front door, he shook his head. "You'll never make it outside." He lifted his right hand far enough out of his pocket for her to see the bright, shiny automatic clenched in his fingers. "This transaction will go much more smoothly if you cooperate. Move, Claire."

Having no choice but to follow his orders, she turned and walked toward the rear of the shop, her entire body trembling. The steady crunch of glass and charred debris beneath his feet told her Navarro stayed close behind her.

Her palms tingled. Her skin got hot and then very cold. She could feel her heart pounding as panic threatened to close in.

She forced herself to swallow over the fear that lodged in her throat. If she let herself panic, she was a goner. *You're not helpless,* she reminded herself. Jackson had taught her self-defense moves. She'd even delivered a blow to his temple that had him bending over at the waist, fighting for air.

If she did it once, she could do it again.

"Stop, and keep your back toward me," Navarro ordered when he had followed her into the back room. The space she used for an office was small, with only a desk, chair and file cabinet. "Now, slide the paper out of your pocket and lay it on the desk."

Claire did as instructed. She couldn't see him, but she heard him step closer, felt the air stir when he retrieved the parchment off the desk.

Was he going to shoot her in the back? Realizing she might have little chance of defending herself, a moment of sheer terror took her, making her so weak she could hardly draw breath. Standing there, waiting, she had the sick sensation that her life was ticking away.

"Turn around, Claire."

When she did, she saw that Navarro had paused several feet from her and the parchment was no longer in sight. His lips were pulled back, his teeth looking snowy against his dark hair and olive skin.

"All my senses told me this document wound up hidden somewhere in your building," he said smoothly. "It's satisfying to know I was right."

"The signatures on the deed give it historical value." She heard the nerves in her voice, but couldn't help it. "But don't you consider holding a gun on me to get your hands on it a little extreme?"

"Not when this is something I've searched for almost my entire life," Navarro said, patting his breast pocket where he now had the parchment. "My great-grand-mother used to tell me stories about a long-lost deed written to her great-great-grandfather by General Santa Anna. Because of Miguel Navarro's distinguished brav-ery while serving under the general at the Alamo, Santa

Anna granted my family ownership of several large tracts of land in Texas."

"I seem to recall that not long after the battle of the Alamo, Sam Houston kicked the general's butt at San Jacinto." Claire shifted against the corner of the desk. The movement put her a step closer to Navarro. A step closer to a chance at defending herself. "That would make all land deeds written by Santa Anna worthless."

Navarro sent her a self-indulgent smile. "I have no delusions Texas will cede me that land. What I want is retroactive payment of the mineral rights attached to it. You see, that particular land encompasses huge oil reserves. Millions are due the Navarro family, and the Santa Anna deed proves it."

"Do you really believe after all this time you'd have any claim to the mineral rights?"

"An attorney has assured me that numerous obscure laws from the 1800s remain in the Texas State Statute. For various reasons they've been overlooked. Several of them have to do with the ceding of mineral rights. The attorney is certain a claim made by the Navarro family, with supporting documentation, will be upheld."

Every second that passed with her eyes fastened on the gun's barrel had Claire's heart picking up its rhythm. She had to keep Navarro talking until she figured out how to get close enough to deliver a blow.

"I'm curious about a few things, so maybe you'll indulge me?"

He moved his shoulders in elegant agreement. "Why not?"

"Why did you suspect I had the deed when I had no idea it even existed?"

"Through a sequence of events. For years I've paid acquaintances to keep their eyes open for the document. One was a man employed by a company that oversees estate sales. He phoned recently from southern California, saying he'd spotted the deed in a stack of legal papers to be offered for sale the next morning. Because of tight security, my man couldn't smuggle the parchment out, so we agreed he would slip it inside the damaged binding of a certain children's book that could be bought for a few dollars. By the following morning, I had another one of my representatives in place to purchase the book. However, when the sale opened, it was gone. I learned later that right after our phone call, my man who worked for the estate-sale company suffered a fatal heart attack."

The dead man, Claire realized, was the employee of Charles's friend, Leon Lovett. And Lovett had allowed Charles to purchase items at the estate sale the night before its official opening.

"My representative later learned the book had been purchased by that damned thief, Charles McDougal." Navarro's tone had gone hard. Hard and cold.

"Charles wasn't a thief."

Pure hatred flickered in Navarro's eyes. "To spite me, McDougal purposely competed against me for items he knew I wanted but which had no worth to him."

Claire thought about the President Andrew Jackson letters Charles had tried to obtain for his terminally ill wife. Navarro had pulled strings to buy them out from under Charles, then refused to sell them for any price.

"My representative also learned that all the items McDougal bought, except for a stack of legal documents, were shipped here to Home Treasures."

Claire flexed her fingers. "Would your representative's name be Ike Bolton?"

"It would," Navarro confirmed. "He was one of many foster children my wife's do-gooding family took in over the years. Bolton showed up last year at our home, needing money. With his criminal past, he was ideal for performing certain jobs I needed done in a discreet manner."

"Like killing people?"

"I didn't order Bolton to murder anyone," Navarro replied, the smoothness returning to his voice. "He came here, intending to buy the books McDougal had shipped to you. However, your shop was closed for the day. Knowing how anxious I was to obtain the hidden deed, Bolton simply broke in. When your handyman interrupted his search and started yelling for the police, Bolton had no choice but to slash his throat."

"No choice?" Claire countered. "Silas was an old man. Bolton could have gagged him. Tied him up."

"Yes, that was unfortunate, but Ike isn't known for restraint. Which is why he returned here that night, intending to break in again. But he spotted your Mr. Castle loitering outside." Navarro pursed his mouth. "Tell me, Claire, are you and Castle lovers? Is that why your engagement with Brice Harrison went by the wayside?"

She ignored the question. "So, because Bolton failed

at getting the books, you came here the following day to see if you'd have better luck."

"Yes. But the land deed wasn't hidden inside the binding of the damaged book you sold me. Or any of the other books I purchased from you that day. Which led me to believe my man on the inside had been unable to retrieve the Santa Anna deed before the heart attack took his life. Since McDougal bought all other legal documents from the estate sale, it was possible he had the deed in his possession. I ordered Bolton to track him down."

"And kill him."

"Again, I gave no such order. Bolton acted on his own. When he searched McDougal's RV, Bolton found a copy of a letter McDougal wrote to a man he hired to translate the documents. Bolton called the translator who told him he had mailed everything to you."

"So, then you sent Bolton back here."

"I instructed him to search the building when it was unoccupied. But you and Castle interrupted the search and Bolton died during the struggle.

"I must tell you, Claire, I have spent anxious moments trying to figure out a way to obtain the document that wouldn't raise your suspicion. I was still working out a plan this morning when I heard about the fire. The possibility that the deed I've sought so long was lost forever made me physically ill. I *had* to come see for myself how much of the building was burned."

Navarro gestured with the automatic, sending the scent of gun oil through the air. "How fortunate for me that I walked in right after you found the deed. And that I overheard you on the phone. Until that moment, I wasn't aware that Bolton had been foolish enough to hint to you what he was after. In the minds of the police, my surname being in the deed could link me to Bolton, however circumstantially. And to the murders he committed. That's a little too close for comfort, Claire. I'm sure you understand why I can't allow you to live."

Her heart hammered and her pulse thundered in her ears. She knew her only chance of survival was to act. Navarro had ordered Bolton to do his bidding because of greed. She was going to try to save herself by feeding on that.

"There's one flaw in your story."

"That would be?"

"General Santa Anna signed more than one deed with Miguel Navarro."

Navarro's eyes filled with a mix of surprise and speculation. "I've only ever heard about one."

"Well, over the past decades someone got their facts wrong. Because yesterday, when it was raining, business was slow, so for the first time I had a chance to go through the documents Charles had the translator mail me."

Her thoughts whirling, Claire made up the lie as she went. "I noted your surname in a deed, but right after I saw it, some customers came in. I put all the documents away for safekeeping. Later, the fire started. I forgot about seeing the deed until the hidden drawer on the chest opened and the second deed popped out."

"*Two* deeds," Navarro breathed. Claire could almost see the dollar signs in his eyes. "Give me the other one."

"It's behind you," she said. "In the closet under the staircase. In my new safe."

He flicked a look over his shoulder. "What's the combination?"

"There isn't one. The lock is activated by touch and voice. Meaning, I have to press my palm on a scanning screen at the same time I say my password into a speaker."

"Then do it."

Dragging in a deep breath, Claire took two steps forward. She didn't have to fake the way her body shook. She was so scared, she wasn't sure her legs were going to continue to support her.

When Navarro didn't move, she said, "You'll need to let me pass."

His eyes narrowed, glinting dully. "You're going to walk to the safe, open it, then back away."

And then you'll shoot me. Her skin prickled with fear as she curled her hands into fists. Navarro was big, tall. Muscular. She had to take him by surprise, it was her only hope.

When he shifted sideways, she stepped forward. With prayers screaming in her head, she stomped her heavy work boot on his instep while sweeping her elbow up against the bridge of his nose. She heard bone crunch, saw blood spurt.

Navarro howled and bent double. She chopped the side of her hand against the back of his neck. He went down on one knee.

Aware he'd kept his grip on the gun, Claire spun toward the door. And caught blurred movement at the corner of her eye.

"What the hell?"

For an instant, she thought she'd conjured up Jackson's image racing toward her. But when he gripped her arms, she realized he was flesh and blood.

"He's got a gun!" She barely got out the words before Jackson shoved her toward the door.

She took two steps into the shop and grabbed a heavy pewter candlestick, intending to supply backup if Jackson needed it. She dashed back into the office in time to see Navarro hit the floor.

She hadn't heard the blow. Jackson didn't even seem to be breathing hard. But now he had the gun in one hand, standing over the unconscious museum curator.

Still holding the candlestick like a weapon, Claire stared at Jackson, her lungs heaving. "I…"

His gaze held hers as he slid the automatic into his waistband and moved to her.

"You can put that down now." He took the candlestick from her gently. "I appreciate the thought."

Claire's knees began to shake, so she locked them stiff. "What are you doing here?"

"I forgot something." He pulled her into his arms. "How about I call Liz and let her deal with the garbage on the floor?"

Claire pressed her face to his throat and willed herself to stop trembling. "Fine. Okay."

Chapter 14

Standing on the building's rooftop, Jackson knew he would forever remember the image of Claire prepared to do battle against Navarro, her knuckles white as bone against the heavy pewter candlestick she'd gripped like a Louisville Slugger. Valiant color had ridden high on her cheeks and determination had glazed her eyes.

He was an idiot a hundred times over for leaving her again.

That realization had nothing to do with how close she'd come to taking a bullet from Navarro's automatic. The truth had first hit him while he'd sat at the airport's boarding gate. It had struck again with the force of a sledgehammer when he'd pried Claire's fingers off the candlestick, wrapped her in his arms and felt resistance.

Since then, the sick certainty that he'd walked away from her one too many times had kept his gut in knots.

"So, my theory is, the General Santa Anna deed must have been mixed in with the other Spanish legal documents Charles McDougal bought at the California estate sale."

Liz Scott's voice dragged Jackson's thoughts back to the business at hand. After a patrol cop had hustled the museum curator off in handcuffs, the detective had suggested they relocate to the building's rooftop terrace where the air was free of smoke. Now, Liz and Claire sat at the wrought-iron table where the angled umbrella in its center provided shade from the late-afternoon sun. Pots of flowers bloomed around the edges of the rug, scenting the warm air with a heady bouquet.

Claire nodded. "When Charles saw both the Navarro name and the general's in the deed, he would have realized he had something of value, if only to Adam Navarro."

"Whom he hated with a passion," Jackson added as he settled into the chair beside Claire's. "Charles had to figure Navarro had as many contacts working estate sales and auctions looking out for certain documents as he did himself. So, in case Navarro had someone on the inside at that estate sale who had spotted the deed, Charles put it in what he assumed was a safe place."

"A hidden drawer in an antique chest, which he shipped here," Liz said, shifting her gaze back to Claire. "He told you he had a potential buyer for the chest, which assured him you wouldn't sell it before he drove back here and reclaimed the deed."

Claire shook her head. "Now, he and poor old Silas are dead because of that piece of paper. So is Ike Bolton."

"And Navarro will do jail time," Liz said. "The reason your call went to my voice mail was I was in chambers with the bleeding-heart judge whom I finally convinced to sign the papers to unseal Bolton's juvie records. I'm betting when I do, the name of Navarro's wife's family will be listed as one of his foster homes."

Liz slid her small notebook into the pocket of her crisp white blazer then squeezed Claire's hand. "You doing okay now?"

"It's going to take me a while to figure that out."

"Understandable." Liz flipped her coppery braid across one shoulder. "Time for me to head to the cop shop and interview Navarro."

As Liz stood, Claire said, "I'll be at your place tonight. How about we get Allie to join us and binge on pizza and wine? My treat."

Jackson's stomach clutched and he caught the look Liz flicked him. Clearly, Claire didn't intend to leave the evening open for him. That was the tricky thing about life, he thought. Too often you didn't know what was impor-tant until it slipped through your fingers.

"Pizza, wine and girl talk sound wonderful." Liz held out her hand to him. "No offense, Special Agent Castle, but I'm getting damn tired of dealing with you in an official capacity."

Jackson returned her handshake. "Likewise, Detec-tive Scott."

To give himself time to settle, he watched until Liz disappeared through the door to the stairwell. Then he shifted his chair to face Claire's. There were shadows in her eyes, he realized. Shadows of the wound he had dealt her.

"There are some things I'd like to say," he said quietly. "Things I need to say."

"There are things I need to say, too," she said in a voice strained taut with emotion. "I should have said them this morning before you left. I just didn't realize what all needed to be dealt with until after you were gone."

He faced lethal danger on an almost daily basis, but her cool, polite tone speared the type of fear through him that he'd never felt before. The palms of his hands went clammy. She was going to end things. For good, this time.

He dipped his head. "Guess you'd better go first, then."

"I thought I could do this. But I can't." Claire had to look away. It hurt too much to look into Jackson's eyes and know she would never see him again. "I can't spend the rest of my life watching you come and go."

She pressed her fingertips against her eyelids. He had to leave, she thought. He had to leave now, before she started weeping. "Jackson, no matter how I feel about you, I don't have the ability to watch you walk in and out of the door and not record the scars."

His throat was raw. "Look at me, Claire. Dammit, look at me."

When her gaze shot back to his face, he curled his hands into fists to keep from touching her. "What you're saying is, you'd rather have no life with me at all?"

"Yes." She eased out a long breath. "We've already said goodbye once today. That's all I'm up for. You came back here because you forgot something, and I'm sure you have another flight you need to catch soon. I'm going to just sit up here for a while and collect my thoughts. So if you could just get whatever it is you forgot and go…."

"…and never darken your doorstep again," he finished.

"We don't work. Our lives don't mesh. We can't be what the other needs, we both know that. It's over, Jackson."

Panic spiraled through him. Christ, what if he was too late? What the hell was he going to do if he could not convince her to give him this one last chance? "What I know is, nothing's been the same since you left me two years ago. I spent the entire time feeling empty and miserable without you. But I didn't come after you because I was afraid."

She went still, her eyes widening. "Afraid? *You*, afraid?"

"Of failure. You'd tried to live in my world, but you couldn't. Just the thought of giving up my job and putting down roots in one place put knots in my gut. I knew if I tried it and it didn't work out, I'd fail not only myself, but you. So I stayed away because I thought I could. Because I thought that was right and fair and best for both of us. I couldn't see any percentage in risking both our futures when you'd certainly be better off with someone else."

"What about you, Jackson? Didn't you think you'd be better off with someone else?"

"Sometimes I told myself I would be. Then I remembered how alive you made me feel. Happy. And I knew I was never going to feel that way again without you. You're who I wanted. Who I've always wanted."

Tears welled in her eyes, clogged her throat. "This

isn't getting us anywhere. How we feel about each other doesn't change our basic needs. We'll never be able to pretend it does."

"Needs change. Evolve," he countered, fighting against the rigid panic in his stomach. "Before, it didn't matter how much I loved you. I was too single-minded and zealous about going after bad guys. Staying in one place would have stopped me from doing that, so I wouldn't even consider changing my lifestyle. I was still thinking that way earlier today when I got the call about Kaddur. I wanted to go after the bastard. Take him down for killing Garrett. And stepping aside to let someone else do that was out of the question."

"I can't imagine you don't still feel that way."

"I didn't know how I felt, *really felt,* until I was sitting at the airport boarding gate."

His panic grew at the thought he was too late. That she'd totally closed her heart to him. If he had to beg, he'd beg. If he had to fight, he'd fight. But he wasn't going to lose her again.

"I was on my way to settle a score with a terrorist, but for the first time, my upcoming mission wasn't on my mind. All I could think about was when I got back here. Back to you. *Home* with you."

She shook her head. "Thinking about coming back doesn't change anything."

"You're right. If you and I are going to have any kind of future together, it has to be built on a new foundation. Which is why when I walked out of the airport, I didn't come directly here. I detoured by the Institute for the Prevention of Terrorism."

"Why did you go there?"

"Tom Iverson at Homeland Security mentioned there was an instructor's position open. Law-enforcement agencies from all over the world send their people here for training. I'll be instructing the guys who go after terrorists like Kaddur."

Claire stared at him. "*You'll* be instructing?"

"Instructing, giving workshops. Teaching surveillance techniques, hands-on self-defense, among other things."

"Jackson, you've never stayed in one place for long."

"There was never a reason to. Now there is. At least, I hope there is." He reached out, gripped her hand. "When we were together before, you were the one who did all the compromising. You gave up your home, your life here. You left Charles, whom you loved. All to be with me. I gave up nothing for you."

He gazed out at the city's skyline, lit by the sun's golden glow. He could be happy here. Content. "I had another thought while I was sitting at the airport today," he continued. "It was about the North Star." He looked back at her. "That's what you are to me, Claire. My constant. My home."

She shook her head. "Jackson, don't."

"Dammit, don't tell me it's too late. Don't tell me you won't give me another chance." He tightened his grip on her hand. "Please don't tell me that."

The pressure in her chest almost burst Claire's heart. "I *can't* give you another chance."

"Claire—"

"Because you never had taken the first one. Until now." She pulled her bottom lip between her teeth. "Do you mean it, Jackson? Do you really think you can stay here?"

"Yes. With you, yes." He felt the first true spark of hope. "I can't go back to the way it's been the past two years. I can't go forward without you."

"We'll have a home?" She felt disbelief give way to hope. "A home we make together?"

"Yes."

"Jackson." She could barely get his name past the tears clogging her throat.

"Say yes, Claire. Give me another chance. Give us another chance. I love you." He tugged her out of her chair and onto his lap. "I've always loved you."

"I love you, too. I can't stop. I've tried."

"Glad you didn't succeed," he said, cupping her cheek in his palm. Everything he needed was right there, in her eyes. "I'm going to stay here, Claire. Be my family. My home."

"Yes." She pressed her mouth to his, and for the first time, she felt an easing of the hard, aching emptiness that had settled inside her when she'd left him two years ago.

Inching her head back, she gazed into the face of the man she loved. The man she'd thought she would have to give up again. The man who'd come back to stay.

She blinked back tears as she linked her fingers with his. "Welcome home, Jackson Castle."

* * * * *

Mills & Boon® Intrigue brings you a thrilling glimpse of Lisa Child's Haunted…

Ariel Cooper has a secret: she can see ghosts. For years Ariel's been hiding it from her powerful, brooding fiancé, David, afraid that he wouldn't understand. Can she trust the man she plans to spend eternity with?

Don't miss this exciting read, available next month in Mills & Boon® Intrigue!

Haunted

by

Lisa Child

Barrett, Michigan, 2006

The wailing sirens and shouting voices receded to a faint hum as the light flashed before Ariel's eyes. Glowing through a thin veil of mist, bright but not blinding, it granted her such clarity that she could see what others could not.

The little girl. Her big, dark eyes wide in her pale face, her black hair hanging in limp curls around her cheeks and over her shoulders. In that pale yellow dress she'd favored, she was dressed for school. But she wasn't there, safe in Ariel's second-grade classroom. Not now. She hovered before the ramshackle house, back from the curb where police cars and an ambulance blocked the street.

Ariel had left her Jeep farther down the road and walked to the house, which sat on the edge of commercial property, only businesses and warehouses surrounding it and a handful of other rundown rental houses. No trees. No grass. No yard in which a child could play. Ariel had ducked under the crime scene tape roping off the property. She didn't need to rush around like all the other people, the ones trying to figure out what had happened or how to help. Before she'd even arrived, she'd known what had happened and that it was too late for help.

As she blinked back tears, the mist thickened and the light faded, dimly shining on just the little girl, who, too, was fading and dissolving into the mist. Ariel reached out a hand, trying to hold on to her, trying to keep her from leaving. Her voice thick with emotion, she whispered the child's name, "Haylee…"

The little girl whispered back, her mouth moving with words Ariel couldn't hear. What did she want to tell her? Goodbye?

The tears fell now, sliding down Ariel's cheeks, blurring Haylee from her vision. "I'm not ready to let you go…."

She was too young to be alone. Only eight. And she'd get no older now.

Ariel's heart ached so much she trembled with the pain. As she shook, the charm dangling from the bracelet on her wrist swayed back and forth. Her hand was still extended, reaching for Haylee as the child faded away. Ariel's fingers clutched at the mist, slipping through the gossamer wisps until she touched something solid. Something strong and warm.

Arms closed around her. A hand pressed her face against a hard shoulder. On a gasping breath, she drew in the rich scent of leather and man. *Her man.*

Even with her eyes closed, she saw David as vividly as if she were staring up at him. Although she wasn't petite at five ten, David towered above her and everyone else. With his golden hair and dark eyes, he was a throwback to the conquering Vikings of centuries ago, not so much in appearance as attitude. Or perhaps a black knight, for he was dressed all in black today—black leather jacket, black silk shirt and black pants.

His deep voice rumbled as he told her, "You shouldn't be here. I'm going to take you home."

"H-how did you know?" she asked. How did he always know where she was and when she needed him? She hadn't called him. She should have. She realized that as she glanced up at his face, his square jaw taut and hard, his dark eyes guarded. But she'd called Ty McIntyre instead—for his badge, not his support.

"Did Ty call you?" Of course the police officer would have called David. They'd been best friends since they were little kids—or so they'd told her. She hadn't known either man that long, just long enough to fall for David.

"Ty's here?" David asked. "Oh, my God, is he the injured officer?"

Ariel blinked the last of the mist away. As it vanished, the faint hum she heard morphed into a cacophony of sirens and shouts. For the first time since arriving on the scene, she became aware of the reporters shouting out questions from the curb as officers held them back. "Mr. Koster, why are you here? What's your involvement?"

Her. If Ty hadn't called David, the live coverage of the scene must have been how he'd known where she was. She didn't ask him, though, because he'd started toward the house. Unlike the media, the officers never attempted to stop him. Everyone knew the richest man in Barrett, Michigan.

They didn't know her. Until David's appearance, neither the police nor the reporters had really noticed her.

"Who is that with you?" a reporter called out

now as Ariel followed David, his shadow falling across her.

"Who's the redhead?" another one shouted.

David ignored them, intent on the house, its door gaping open on broken hinges.

"Ty's hurt?" she asked him, her voice cracking. She never would have called him had she known it would put him in danger.

"I don't know. I have to find him," David said, then glanced down at her. "But I don't want you to come inside the house."

His dark eyes soft with concern, he obviously feared what she might see. If he only knew… But that was perhaps the only thing he didn't know about her—what she saw. She couldn't tell him because she couldn't explain what she didn't understand herself.

"I'll be all right," she promised him. It was an empty promise because she had no way of knowing if she spoke the truth. No way of knowing what might happen next. That gift had been her mother's, not hers.

He must have assumed she meant she'd be okay by herself outside, for he withdrew his arm and started toward the gaping door. But before he could step inside, two men filed out wearing medical examiner's jackets and carrying a small black body bag on a gurney between them.

Would she surrender to the sheikh?

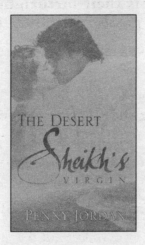

Possessed by the Sheikh by **Penny Jordan**

After being stranded in the desert, Katrina was rescued by a sheikh and taken back to his luxury camp. The sheikh thought Katrina little more than a whore. And then he discovered that she was a virgin… Now he must marry her!

Prince of the Desert by **Penny Jordan**

One hot night in the kingdom of Zuran has left Gwynneth fevered and unsure. Gwynneth doesn't realise she shared a bed with Sheikh Tariq bin Salud – and he is determined to claim her virginity…

Available 18th July 2008

www.millsandboon.co.uk

M&B

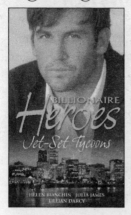

Celebrate 100 years of pure reading pleasure with Mills & Boon®

To mark our centenary, each month we're publishing a special 100th Birthday Edition. These celebratory editions are packed with extra features and include a FREE bonus story.

Plus, you have the chance to enter a fabulous monthly prize draw. See 100th Birthday Edition books for details.

Now that's worth celebrating!

July 2008

**The Man Who Had Everything
by Christine Rimmer**
Includes FREE bonus story *Marrying Molly*

August 2008

Their Miracle Baby by Caroline Anderson
Includes FREE bonus story *Making Memories*

September 2008

Crazy About Her Spanish Boss by Rebecca Winters
Includes FREE bonus story
Rafael's Convenient Proposal

Look for Mills & Boon® 100th Birthday Editions at your favourite bookseller or visit
www.millsandboon.co.uk

4 FREE

BOOKS AND A SURPRISE GIFT!

We would like to take this opportunity to thank you for reading this Mills & Boon® book by offering you the chance to take FOUR more specially selected titles from the Intrigue series absolutely FREE! We're also making this offer to introduce you to the benefits of the Mills & Boon® Reader Service™—

- ★ FREE home delivery
- ★ FREE gifts and competitions
- ★ FREE monthly Newsletter
- ★ Exclusive Reader Service offers
- ★ Books available before they're in the shops

Accepting these FREE books and gift places you under no obligation to buy, you may cancel at any time, even after receiving your free shipment. Simply complete your details below and return the entire page to the address below. You don't even need a stamp!

YES! Please send me 4 free Intrigue books and a surprise gift. I understand that unless you hear from me, I will receive 6 superb new titles every month for just £3.15 each, postage and packing free. I am under no obligation to purchase any books and may cancel my subscription at any time. The free books and gift will be mine to keep in any case.

18ZED

Ms/Mrs/Miss/Mr ....Initials ....
BLOCK CAPITALS PLEASE

Surname ....

Address ....

....

....Postcode ....

Send this whole page to:
UK: FREEPOST CN81, Croydon, CR9 3WZ